The Losers

Alexa Winter

WESTBOW
PRESS®
A DIVISION OF THOMAS NELSON
& ZONDERVAN

for my favorite yorgi love Jen. ... FOR HOPE Alexa Winter

WestBow Press books may be ordered through booksellers or by contacting:

WestBow Press
A Division of Thomas Nelson & Zondervan
1663 Liberty Drive
Bloomington, IN 47403
www.westbowpress.com
1 (866) 928-1240

ISBN: 978-1-9736-1407-4 (sc)
ISBN: 978-1-9736-1406-7 (hc)
ISBN: 978-1-9736-1408-1 (e)

Library of Congress Control Number: 2018900285

Print information available on the last page.

WestBow Press rev. date: 01/26/2018

For everyone who has lost

Death never comes at the right time, despite what mortals believe. Death always comes like a thief.
—Christopher Pike

1

Jane

The air hung motionless in my throat. I could never quite exhale until I heard the now-familiar phrase: "I am so sorry for your loss." Only then would the air rush out, with pain flooding its surface.

"Really?" I wanted to shout. My heart wanted to spit out the incredulous response: "Are you really sorry? Did you even know her? Did you ever see her? Do you have any idea how much I lost?"

I was forced to suppress my exasperation, though. Because, after all, the unsuspecting Walmart clerk had not asked for me to come through checkout lane 7. And certainly, it was not written into the Walmart Employee Handbook: "How to Deal with a Customer Who Just Watched Her Mom Die."

I was completely affronted by the most casual conversation now. "How are you?" seemed like a threat. "How have you been?" was a call to arms. And "What's been going on?" Well, that was a question that completely freaked me out. I had been plucked out of the humdrum of everyday life and let loose in a storm of emotional run-for-your-life. I felt as if the rest of the world moved in this careless, slow-motion film, while my own horror flick of a life raced after me and hunted me down.

It took my last ounce of kindness to say to the Walmart clerk—whose name, I could see by her banal white tag, was Diane—"Yes,

I am sorry too." I could not say, "Thank you." I could not say, "It's okay." Because, clearly, it was not okay. And to be honest, I was not thankful that she felt sorry. I actually despised her for her seemingly stable mental state. I feigned a solidarity with my fate, averted her eyes, grabbed my flimsy plastic bag with the week's necessities for survival, and waded out of the checkout lane into the sea of shoppers coming and going.

I ran over my short list: some garish plastic toy for my three-year-old, some food for her to eat, and something for our dogs to eat—or was it the cats? I hoped I had remembered it all. I was only a few strides from the cashier, and I had already started questioning whether I was walking out with what I had come for. My mind often played these tricks on me now. And my body would sometimes play along.

Just moments ago, in the grocery section, I had stopped involuntarily. Suddenly, I had been unsure as to how to continue. I had wondered, *Should I keep walking? Or not? Why am I even at Walmart? How can I get out of here? Who are these people, who all radiate this casual vibe—as if going to Walmart were pleasant?*

Once again, I had felt like a fugitive of the la-di-da who had fled into the unrelenting grip of misery. Again, it had come, the fatalistic thought: *How can I ever possibly escape from here?*

And the question which followed: *Do I mean Walmart, or do I mean from my life?*

The cart had been my only support. I had stared at it and gripped it like an old person's walker. I was stuck in aisle 14. An ocean of panic had started to erode my reason as the grimy, snow-trodden floor of the store monopolized my gaze. I had found myself with no will to move forward. I had blinked my eyes, a feeble attempt to break loose from my frozen state.

And then she had materialized. A tiny little girl had tucked herself onto the bottom shelf of the cereals. I saw her out of the corner of my eye. The stock was low, and she had been able to plug herself into the display, lay on her back, and grin up at her mom with a crazy, mischievous little look—teeth just coming in and courage just

2

pouring out, brave without realizing her own vulnerability. I had been struck by that little girl's look—not really meant for me—and it had ignited some sort of motion within me. The reference was obvious. I had one of those at home who was waiting for me; the intuitive force to move on had kicked in. Then, I had been able to feel my limbs, and I had desperately groped for my list.

"Come on," I had mumbled to myself. "Move on to the next thing."

Macaroni and cheese. Surely, I could find the little blue-and-yellow box and place it in my cart. I had reassured myself and picked up my back foot.

These types of episodes had become the new normal, although they made me feel about as abnormal as I ever had. When I finally reached the car, I had played the list over several times and resolved that I had gotten it all. I crawled out of the Walmart parking lot. These days, this was as scary to me as traversing any six-lane highway in Houston or navigating the puzzle of highways through St. Louis. It was just a few years back, when I was still travelling full time for work, I had sped over those roadways with such ease. Such abandon. Life was so unadulterated then. I had known no tragedy. I had witnessed plenty of tragic death, but only as an accessory. I had been a spectator or even down on the sidelines, cheering someone else on. But never with flesh in the game—where there are no distractions available, only waiting out the formidable clock. I knew now: Truly knowing tragedy is living in it without one second of escape. It's not like showing up for someone who is going through it—say, stopping at a funeral or bringing a dish to someone's home—because even then, you can go home. You might still feel sorry, but you are not lost in the chaos of the trauma yourself.

Back in my innocent days, I had not truly known tragedy. I was self-assured. I thought I was bigger than the chaos of the world and I wandered around the U.S. proving it. I walked through the crack ghettos of Miami after getting off the train from work; I jumped in any cab on any street in Philadelphia and headed for any neighborhood I chose, without consideration for the fragility of life itself. And now, here I was, crawling through the Walmart parking lot in Fenton, Michigan. Timid and inhibited. And just hoping to make it to my house. Two miles at the most. "Oh, how the mighty have fallen," as my mom used to say. That is, until the cancer treatment dragged her into the ICU and the ventilator made speech impossible. She had only spoken with her eyes after that.

One more mile to go. I was driving down the main road now. There were just two major turns remaining. In the left-hand turn lane, waiting, I became fixated on the cars coming at me, and it happened again. I was lost, and I started to lose sensation in my torso. My breathing froze. I had no forward motion thoughts or inclinations. No one beeped behind me. And I thought, *Who would care if I just sat here for a while?*

This exact street, which could have been Main Street, USA, had been the setting for moments from my idyllic childhood. I opened that satchel to peer in now. Might as well take a walk down memory lane—I certainly was not about to take the left turn down the side street.

Freedom Park, which was snuggled up between the street I was on and one that branched off from it, was the perfect island for families to abandon themselves to watching the Fourth of July parade. I could see myself thirty years ago: flitting around with a wooden-handled US flag, flailing in the grass, the long-awaited sunny days, gearing up to see my big brother play the drums in the city's high school band. This pretty city park stood resolute in front of me, unaware of my gawking now. Reminiscing, I could almost feel the sticky tar beneath my bare feet as I ran out for Tootsie Rolls and ran back into the smell of my mom's flowery summer perfume. I would throw the Tootsie Rolls into my stash under her lawn chair and head back out for more loot.

And then there was the home, just down the street on the left. My best friend in middle school had been Jessie Washburn. And her family had lived there. It was a grand old Victorian home, which at the time had been amid renovation. It had stood out, even on a street lined with grand old homes. The Washburns' home was the prettiest of all. Maybe the most austere and yet feminine in some way. Back in middle school, we would spend hours in Jessie's second-floor bedroom, watching the cars below, playing the "The Next Car Is Your Future Car" game. And now, I was in one of those cars. And the future I had found myself in was nothing like a childhood dream.

The innocence and hopefulness of those days long ago began to melt back into the hard truth and my stark reality—stuck in the left-hand turn lane, too scared to move, because movement meant I was still alive. Alive in the forlorn circumstance I had found myself in—in the wake of my mom's death, during a separation with my husband—and I could not begin to imagine an escape from it. Except for the one thing that I figured was the only quick way out. To just slip away myself. In some sort of nonpainful, quiet fashion. But this thought was always interrupted by the image of Gwin, my one and only child. She needed me.

I was thirty-seven now and was fighting with every ounce of my spirit to go on without my mom. But Gwin, she was three. I simply could not wreak that havoc into her life. Or so I told myself—most of the time. The thought of ending my life early was ever present. And sitting here in the road, I began to mull it over once again. My goal was simply to be absent from the present. Who cared about the process of becoming absent? I could figure that out. One more story problem in the story of my life, I reassured myself.

And then, something interrupted my planning; a whisper: "Janey, you have to turn and go home now."

It was not my own voice. It was hers. No one else ever called me "Janey." Only my mom. An involuntary reflex kicked in. The accelerator pedal was not all that far away. My right foot reached for it.

But how could I have heard her voice?

Dead people didn't talk; this was one thing I was still certain of. *No matter*, I thought. I took the left and made my way home.

Tawly

If someone walking by could see Tawly, they might describe her as an angelic-looking warrior. But people on earth could not: see her, that is. If they did notice anything, she would appear as rays of light or what they might describe as a sun spot, but they would never actually see her. Not now, now that she belonged to the Next Place. In Tawly's life on earth, she had been a demure and petite woman, and her name had been Iris. She was self-described as shy, borderline reclusive. She had been very pretty, with eyes that showed up before she did, warming you up to her before she was a breath away. That calming aura always preceded her and followed her. Many would say they felt more at peace when they were simply in the same room as her.

But in the Next Place, a person was fashioned differently. Your appearance was not born of flesh and bone and family genetics, but rather from the seat of your soul. Those things people nurtured in their hearts on earth would be a blueprint for their presence in the Next Place, which came after life on earth. Here, Tawly had many of the same distinguishing features she had on earth, such as her eyes, but the essence of who she was had been drawn according to the life she had lived in the First Place. And so it was that for those who met her now, she appeared both terrifying and beautiful, and simultaneously felt like a safe harbor. She emanated a daffodil-colored light, flecked with gold, which appeared like an aura around her. Tawly's aura was almost blinding. The stronger the heart of a person on earth, the stronger their light in the Next Place. And on earth, Tawly had been like a rebel for justice, packaged up like a Happy Day's princess. However, nowadays, Tawly could be very dangerous. Still, she was unaware of this prowess, as she was still new.

Tawly wanted to be sure that Janey got home. And so, she waited next to the tree, beside Janey's driveway. Waiting was far different for people from the Next Place. She experienced no impatience, as the economy of time was flipped upside down. The true matter was never the amount of time remaining. The true matter was the state of the heart and the outcome. Always the outcome. The outcome was imperative for these types of missions; Tawly's mission was to keep Janey's heart hooked on hope and to keep her alive.

Tawly was what those in the Next Place called a Keeper. A Keeper was assigned to someone who was left behind on earth, left behind after death swallowed up one of their most cherished companions. If a Keeper was assigned, it was because that person who was left behind was on the precipice of taking their own life. They wanted out. People who were left behind and were in danger were called the Losers, and Janey was Tawly's Loser. Before Tawly died, she had been Janey's mother, her friend, and her kindred spirit; now, she was her Keeper.

The Losers, who were all grieving the death of someone they believed they could not live without, were in such tenuous states that their will was often misguided, to the point of self-destruction. They were blinded to the possibility of ever experiencing joy on earth again. And they found no solace in the "time heals all wounds" mantra. How could they? Time had just been forever poisoned for them. Now it was simply time left in an emotional prison. They were walking on high wires. So the Keepers were on a life-or-death mission to tip the scales in the Loser's favor. It was not a given; they did not always win. For the Legion was there as well. And the Legion played by an entirely different set of rules. Their goal was simple and straightforward: to steal life.

To face and defeat the Legion, the Keepers had to use every bit of goodness, knowledge, and light bestowed on them. And their previous time on earth was essential to the task, as well. Upon being assigned to a Loser, the Keeper was given a mantra. When Tawly was assigned to her own daughter, they handed her a piece of paper, which read:

Paint Beauty, Speak Hope, Whisper Eternal Love

Not only did she have the fortune-cookie-like piece of paper, but it was somehow branded on Tawly's heart the day she became Jane's

Keeper, like a tattoo but branded on her soul, instead. Each Keeper was given a different mantra, which was authored for the Loser they were meant to protect. Upon commencement, the Keepers could reject the branding and request a new one. Because, after all, the Keeper's soul was the one which had been woven with their Loser in the former life. There was no one, other than Annais himself, who knew what the Keeper knew about their own Loser, the one they had rightly been chosen to protect. Annais was the ultimate authority of the Next Place, but he could not be bothered with choosing the mantras. He was in a larger battle himself, a battle few understood or were privy to, and so one that was rarely spoken of.

Sitting patiently beside the tree, Tawly repeated these words to herself now: "Paint Beauty, Speak Hope, Whisper Eternal Love."

As she whispered these words, a soft burn of warmth crept from the crown of her head to her feet, alighting the ethereal body Tawly now inhabited. This warmth surged through her newly mended soul, and an idea came to her. Keepers had constant knowledge of their Losers' whereabouts; they could watch them as they moved about the earth. Tawly looked into her vision of Janey. She had about sixty seconds before her daughter would drive around the corner. She must work fast. She chose her colors in a flurry of inspiration: burnt tangerine, the deepest part of the watermelon pink, the slightest bit of moon dusk purple, and a hint of steel gray. And now a pattern to speak to her. Tawly knew that her daughter adored tons of color but preferred hard lines. So she drew an asymmetrical yet whimsical pattern, across an otherwise darkening gray sky, ablaze with these colors. This put a funny grin on Tawly's face. On earth, she had always wondered how each sunset could be so wildly different from the night past. Now she knew: Various Keepers painted sunsets all over the earth. Well, she had painted a pretty striking one, if she did say so herself. She hoped this would stop Janey in her tracks.

Any second now. 7, 6 … 3, 2, 1. The black car loped around the corner like it was being pushed from behind. It was moving with such a ghastly slowness, as if the despondency of the captain made the ship lifeless as well. Tawly recognized Janey's eyes first, searching out of the windshield. She looked absent from her own body, which panged Tawly, but then she saw it happen. The sunset came into view as Janey's car approached the house. There was an instant as Janey's eyes captured the artful sky, and then the life blood sprang back into her countenance. And as the slightest of smiles spread across Janey's face, Tawly was reminded that creating beauty was one of the most powerful tools in her arsenal.

This small victory pleased Tawly. Quite the opposite from what she expected, there were all kinds of emotions now that she was in the Next Place. The difference was that now, the usefulness of each emotion was obvious. A pang of sorrow, like the one when she watched Janey come around the corner, would simply spur Tawly on for the next day. It became fuel for her next intention: another reason to work toward keeping her daughter alive, nothing more. Tawly now felt the surrender that came with having given all her energy to her task. She watched as Janey grabbed the Walmart bags out of the back seat and made her way into the house. Tawly was lucky enough to get a quick glimpse of little Gwin through the door as Janey pushed her way inside to relieve the next-door neighbor, who had agreed to babysit for a short spell.

Gwin's big head of brown curls and face smeared with what must be strawberries peeked through the crack in the door. Tawly thought she might have even looked right at her. Was that possible? Could she see her? Either way, it was enough to put a flat-out smile on Tawly's face. Oh, how she loved being a grandmother. She briefly wondered if she was technically still a grandma, even though she was dead. Her thoughts were getting somewhat wild; she surmised she must be getting tired. And so, she decided she would retire for a spell to her Gathering Place.

2

Tawly

Upon blinking, Tawly found herself in the middle of a lodge-like structure. It was a true work of art, as charming a chalet as her eyes had ever set upon on earth. The place was set down in a wild glade of evergreens. Windows opened floor to ceiling to allow the light of the sky in, and screen like openings permitted the natural smells from outside to cascade in on the wind. Yet there was no evidence of cold, except for the backdrop of falling snowflakes outside. They waxed and waned, but always, they came. Tawly's heart settled as they fell outside. It was meditative to her; the balm of those falling snowflakes soothed any angst she brought back with her. Every detail of her Gathering Place had been painstakingly planned and accommodated. Just for her. But amazingly enough, for some others as well. Long periods of solitude were not allowed in the Next Place. The work was too taxing. No one could be expected to endure it alone.

The details of Tawly's Gathering Place were woven into being during her childhood years on earth, when her name was still Iris. During those years, she would sneak out to the backyard and find sanctuary in the small circle of pine trees in her parents' backyard. When her parents were yelling (or even worse, when their silent treatments would shut the whole house down), she would long for sap-covered fingers, pine streaming through her senses, and a new height to climb to in escape. Although she usually started climbing to get away from her parents' fighting, as she got higher, she would abandon reality altogether. She had found solace and surrender in those trees. Of course, she did not have those words, at those times. But when she had forged that pampering of her own young self, she was also forging the details of the dwelling that would be her future Gathering Place.

Upon arriving at the lodge, Tawly saw a few familiar faces. They were not all Keepers; there were many different roles in the Next Place. Tawly wasn't even sure of all the different groups, but everyone had a job of sorts. There was Raynia: the first Mender she had met in the Next Place. The Menders got to sew together the hurts of one's past life into the tapestry of a person's patched-up heart for the Next Place. Tawly briefly wondered why that couldn't be her job. It seemed much less stressful. She decided to ask someone later.

There were a couple of others across the room, whom Tawly had never seen. Probably other Keepers, she deemed, as they looked exhausted. And one Taker. Tawly shivered just looking at him. His hair was kind of tousled, and his brow was furrowed. He was in the corner with a book, sidled up by the raging fire, which seemed like it jumped out of the actual fireplace, but never seemed to do any damage. She turned away, as she had decided she was going to keep her distance from the Takers. She had concluded that they were a strange bunch. Anyone who had to rip people away from their loved ones (that's the way she currently looked at it) had to be a bit odd. They were very much to themselves, and Tawly had been told that more than anyone, they needed the Gathering Place. And so, they were often here. Although she felt some sympathy for their assignment (maybe it was even more stressful than her own, she mused), Tawly was still reticent to approach them. Maybe she was still a little shaken, thanks to the Taker who had come for her at the hospital, when the life support system had sucked the life right out of her. First, she had been visited by a Messenger, who had warned her that she was about

11

to die. It hadn't seemed but a moment after the Messenger left her with the news, and then Tawly's Taker had come. Tawly just wished one of them had told her what to expect next.

But maybe that would have been too much to bear. To know what it would feel like to be ripped away from earth. To be taken to the Next Place and then to be given a task you would never choose but could hardly even think to refuse: To try and save your own child who was left behind on earth, even though you were no longer there yourself. Yes, if Tawly's Messenger had told her this ... well, she would not have believed it anyhow. Or she might have given up the ghost that very instant, out of sheer terror.

She brushed the thought of her last moments on earth away; there was more pressing business at hand here and now. Just as Tawly had been leaving Janey to return to the Gathering Place, an ominous feeling had struck her. Something dark and disconcerting. So, for now, Tawly shook off the memory of her own death march and the assorted players and decided to look for someone to help her.

First things first, though, she thought.

She headed across the common area of the lodge to grab a cup of freshly prepared java. To her delight, there was always hot, fresh coffee at the lodge. She grabbed a cup, filled it up, and scoured the room for Raynia. She noticed her over by the eastern windows. Tawly figured Raynia was captivated by the snowflakes that were coming in a torrential fashion, backlit by the late evening moon. Tawly could have sat mesmerized by the scene too, but she needed to ask Raynia about the feeling she had when she had left Janey just minutes ago. She had not experienced a feeling like that since she'd gotten to the Next Place, and she wondered if Raynia had any idea what such a dark feeling might have meant.

3

Abaddon

Veiled from Tawly's sight, Abaddon loitered behind the tree across the street from Jane's little home. He raised his head as he heard the approaching whistle of the train. Even though he was seething with anger, he allowed himself to breathe in the surroundings. Not only could he hear the metal train wheels methodically clashing on the tracks, he could also feel the rolling roar of the nearby highway. This spoke to Abaddon's senses. There was so much potential destruction in those sounds, and this pleased him immensely. He glanced over to watch Jane slip into her front door across the backdrop of the circus sunset Tawly had drawn. He spat in disgust as the colors began to fade into his deeply coveted darkness. As dusk settled on him like the heavy cloak he always sought, he allowed his mind to wander back to an earlier assignment many years ago.

Thirty years ago, Tawly had a different name. She was still alive and on earth; back then, Abaddon recalled, she had been called Iris. He had hated her name. It was too pretty and held meaning. Abaddon hated anything with meaning. It was a play on names that her Irish mother had conceived and was eerily poignant, as this was the color of her most prominent and distinctive feature: her eyes. Iris was given to Abaddon with specific instructions: Eliminate her quickly. The

Assigner was clear. Iris was already in a struggle. And she should be finished off; her life should be taken as quickly as possible.

Eventually, Abaddon learned that Iris was indeed underwater in a sea of depression, and the waves had already begun to fill her lungs. She still breathed the air just above the next coming wave, but the rocks of certain destruction were near, and she had been getting closer to them all the time. Abaddon's job would be to finish her off, to ensure the next time she came up for air, he would have a tsunami-size wave waiting for her. The beach of Iris's depression was a familiar saga of the times. She had given so much of her life—her talent and her passion—to her children and her husband. She was often alone, as the children were at school for a good part of the day, and her husband was always at the office. And she would end up roaming from room to room, ruminating on what remained of her life. She was in the folds of what some would call a midlife crisis. Which was a ridiculous name for it. For many, this would be their end-of-life crisis. Her father had been dying of a bad liver, which he medicated with more Pabst Blue Ribbon, and her mom had been dying as well, but more slowly of the less speedy (but just as lethal) perpetual worry. At her lovely suburban home, her three children, Kim, Ron, and Janey, would return each night to a stage that Iris would set. The props would move in cadence as she directed the Home Sweet Home production. Unbeknownst to them, she had been quietly dying backstage between each scene.

To this day, Abaddon still could not figure out why Iris had been so important to get rid of. But it had come from the top of the ranks; she was his assignment, and she was to be taken immediately. Abaddon had watched Iris for a couple of days before he had set to work: mother of a few young children, wife of an on-again off-again workaholic, caretaker for two ailing parents, whom she was constantly trying to save. It was as if she were the lifeguard of the group. She would be a no-brainer, he deduced. Do-gooders had always seemed so silly to Abaddon. He had written her off like a pliable child. He would whisper lies, insults, and accusations in her ear, and she would want to be whisked away from the face of the earth in record time, he had told himself. He had figured he was above such trite altruism.

Well, Iris, in all her simplicity and all her purity, had issued a KO to Abaddon that shocked everyone involved. Iris was the only one who had gotten away from him to date. And to be sure, this made Abaddon hate Tawly here and now. He looked at her and knew he could never have that chance at her again, which was utterly confounding. He smiled now, realizing that disease had finally killed her some three decades later. He briefly wondered who was lucky enough to orchestrate that, but as usual with Abaddon, his thoughts quickly returned to himself. He so wished he could have a "re-do" and try once more to make sure she left well before her time. However, since that small setback with Iris, he had refined his methods and approaches, and now, he figured he was unstoppable.

Abaddon was one of the most relentless Destroyers in the Legion. Each had their specialty, but collectively, the Legion worked like a cancer, earnestly seeking out people at their most vulnerable moments and capitalizing on their weakness to finish them off. Abaddon's method was straightforward and lethal. He did not mess around with relationships or money. He completely avoided disease and accidents. Not to be misunderstood, these were things he liked to watch wreak havoc on people. But his expertise, the pinnacle of his talent, came in washing a person's self-worth away. And oh, the skill he had. It was often whispered in the Legion that Abaddon could wash away an entire army's confidence if he wanted to. Abaddon was likened to a tornado by some. Many in the Legion estimated that the slow-moving, eventual destruction of someone was the most pleasurable—but not Abaddon. He relished seizing on one crucial moment in a person's life. He would cut them to the bone and convince them they need not go on. And then he would play his favorite trick: He would seize their last ally in the fight and sever that tie. With great satisfaction, he would watch as they clambered for their personal life vests, their last ropes. And then he would laugh at their panic, their inability to pull themselves onto the lifeboat. Once they were dead, he would relish the additional notch in his belt.

It was just one more domino set into motion, which he always tried to capitalize on. The path of destruction he could incite was genius in his eyes. When a person was taken from earth too soon, the possibilities were endless. He could sometimes watch an encore of suicides after he orchestrated just one, with little to no intervention. Abaddon's reputation and passion for destruction had caused the rest of the Legion to coin him Rip. He took after his nickname in every fashion. He even looked the part. He was one of the most attractive in the Legion, at least at first glance. His hair was thick and wavy, and his square face spoke of strength. In the Next Place, he towered over the other Destroyers. He was at his prime physically and could wring the neck of any one of his colleagues. As a matter of fact, the more Losers you could steal away from earth, the more strength you appeared to have. He carried a blanket of tattoos, with all the names of those he had stolen away early. He was a walking poster child of menace. Abaddon relished this and wore it like an Unwelcome mat at his front door.

But get close enough and steal a glance into his eyes—which was difficult, as his eyes always seemed to be half closed—and you would see the deteriorating soul that he housed. Every person he stole away bore an ever-increasing cavern into his own soul. This was inevitable. The Legion never told the Destroyers this. It was just part of doing business. Abaddon sensed it each time. But he had yet to equate it to his conquests. And honestly, he did not really care. Abaddon measured himself and his worth according to his physical prowess and his ability to win. Still, there was that one black mark that he could not erase: Iris, who, when she arrived at the Next Place, had been given the new name Tawly. And Iris, who thirty years ago had survived, even when he had done his best to destroy her.

Ah well, she must have had some extra special help, he consoled himself now as he leaned harder into the tree.

She had spoken right back against his threats and had laughed at some of his best insinuations. He had not been able to hold her mentally, and he had kept getting blindsided with interventions from the Other Side. He knew it now: He had greatly underestimated Iris and those he was up against. He had been made an absolute fool. To soothe his ego, he had decided he would bury that memory like a bad dream, until he could remedy the ridicule he felt with some sort of retaliation.

And that time had finally arrived. That time was now. Now, he had been assigned to Jane: Tawly's own daughter. And it was Tawly he would have to beat to eliminate Jane. Perhaps he was not able to destroy Tawly before her time. But Jane: She would be the sacrificial lamb to soothe Abaddon's ego, to allow him to cleanse himself of his one mistake. Tawly could not be removed now, but if Abaddon could make her daughter suffer, and her grandchildren pay, and generations to come lose out on the life Jane had left but would never live out ... well then, he could erase that pockmark off his face.

He could go to the feet of his leader and once and for all show him that he is worthy to be second in command. No one else had ever been as fastidious, as effective, and as heartless as Abaddon. Only one thing plagued him: his inability to get rid of Iris, his one defeat. Defeat was a tough monkey to carry on your back here. Especially if you wanted to carry it to the top. Tawly had put that unwieldy beast on his shoulder. Now, she would pay for it. Someone had found a way to make sure Jane was Abaddon's assignment. Probably some lowly Assigner who hoped Abaddon would repay him with the favor of a greater position, once Abaddon had more authority.

Let him help me, thought Abaddon. *I will repay him by destroying him too; he will never remember me nor my one defeat. I will obliterate any possible notion that I couldn't finish Iris off. Just as soon as I eliminate Jane.*

The prideful lust, which just barely masked his mountainous insecurity, seemed like it might drip right off his chiseled face as he collected himself and refocused on the task at hand: Jane.

Abaddon noted that the babysitter was meandering back to her own home, and across the street, Jane had just turned the light on inside. He could see her moving pragmatically through the house. Kitchen light to make little Gwin dinner. Bathroom light to start little Gwin's bath. Bedroom light to read little Gwin's bedtime story. Gwin's light extinguished. And then nothing. Except for the basement light. After one week of observing Jane, Abaddon knew that, like clockwork, Jane would retreat to the farthest point from Gwin's bedroom and begin her nightly routine of sobbing. He had watched it the last few nights now. It was pathetic. She would writhe, choke, and lie on the floor until she was sopping wet and the dogs were convinced she was dying. She would then shuffle back to her bedroom and collapse with her mom's old shawl: the one Iris had worn during chemo. Abaddon loved that part. Just watching her absolutely exhausted, with no defenses, with no energy, with nothing positive around her or near her. Alone. Abandoned. Desperate. A ball of yarn and hospital memories as her only solace. And oh, so close to defeat.

He could taste her demise already. It hung in the air of her lonely bedroom, and he hadn't lifted a finger yet. Jane's circumstances themselves were enough to push the most sensible person to lunacy. All he would need to do is tweak a little here and there. He sighed as he thought how beneath him this work was, anyhow. He should really be given more important persons now. He still figured this was afforded to him as a vendetta, but he wanted more visibility. Let him knock out someone with great power on earth; maybe that would show his leader what Abaddon was made of.

"Never the matter," he muttered to himself. "I will get rid of this nobody girl and then demand a more notable person." He assuaged his own disappointment with the falsity that he had some sort of control in the Next Place.

And he told himself that this mission could be fun. A little game of cat and mouse. He pictured Tawly. He had to admit her aura was a bit unnerving, and her newly formed body spoke strength and fortitude. But then he imagined how her face might look as her daughter was being destroyed and dying. Those moments were the pinnacle of

Abaddon's job. Whenever Abaddon won and a Keeper lost a Loser, they would give their Loser in hand to the Taker. At this moment, the Keeper would become visible to the Loser. And by taking the Loser's hand, they would have to experience the pain and suffering present at that moment. This was the rumor, anyhow. The Legion could not be present during this exchange. But Abaddon could imagine the agony, and he lusted for it. Abaddon pictured Tawly handing Jane over to one of the Takers and envisioned her excruciating pain at enduring the loss—her own loss, her daughter's loss, her other children's loss, her granddaughter's loss—all on Tawly's shoulders, all at once.

Maybe, Abaddon thought, *it will be so traumatic and fantastic that it will do the unprecedented when I get rid of Jane. Maybe Tawly will somehow be ruined too.*

She could not be ripped from the protection of Annais. This was what Abaddon had been told, anyhow. But maybe, just maybe, something phenomenal would happen, and she could be devastated to the point of becoming irrelevant from here on out.

This was the closest thing Abaddon ever felt to the idea of hope. It was a plagiarized version of true hope, more like the longing of an immature child, like the shallow hope to be a rock star when there was no commitment to cultivating one's talent. A selfish vision of what might be. All about the child. Yes, it was always all about Abaddon. This was not real hope. But he was limited in his understanding. He could only grasp ambition: targeted for self-satisfaction, self-gain, and endless attainment. To those outside the Legion, this eternal searching and nonstop pandering seemed senseless. But it was all he had ever known. He was on a train to nowhere. But he just kept on, getting off at one station and changing tracks. All the while, he was headed for a destination that he could never get to. There was no ETA, and his goal was of no purpose. He was involved in tangential battles for the Legion but thought he was waging his own great war. For sure, he had some measure of impact. He had taken a fair amount of people from the First Place before they should have gone. He had robbed many people of life they had yet remaining. But his impression of his own importance was vastly overwrought.

Now that Tawly had left and Jane's good Samaritan neighbor was back at her own place, Abaddon crossed the road. He sauntered casually, as he knew no one here could see him, unless they were truly looking, which was highly unlikely, especially these days. People in the First Place seemed to be sucked into little devices they carried around, and they barely noticed their own feet in front of them. Surely, they were not keen enough to notice the likes of him. He peered in the front bay window. Although he could not see Jane sobbing, he could hear her. And he could tell she must have been there for a bit now because even the dogs, who were watching her from the kitchen floor, were starting to look concerned.

She's so crazy, even wild animals think she's nuts, Abaddon said to himself, chuckling.

That was enough to satisfy him for now. He would leave her to her own musings for the night. He wanted to toy with her a bit but figured she couldn't even hear him over her own cries. He walked away from the little house and shot over his shoulder:

"Enjoy the safety of the looney bin you live in, for now. I'll be back before you know it."

Annais

Apart from the sporadic crackling of the candle chandelier, which hung from the center of the vaulted ceiling, Annais's office was without sound. There were clouds forming outside the open windows; they were also silent—for now. The windows were propped open, as he knew the storm was coming and was keen on inhaling the smell of the approaching rain. However, because the windows surrounded the second-floor loft area, he left them only slightly ajar. He mused that the foreboding clouds might snake themselves right into the loft. And he did not want to allow the rain to soak the floor. He had precious little time to tidy it up just now. Annais was deep in thought about what the Legion had been up to lately. He was in a conundrum of sorts. And this made him a bit surly.

He looked at the darkening windows from the vantage point of his desk. The construction of this room had a studious vibe to it. It boasted tall ceilings, a loft that ran the circumference of the room, and windows that allowed the natural light to bathe the main room below. There were three rolling ladders, which allowed one to climb into the loft area. The lower level's main attraction was a monstrous fireplace just opposite from Annais's desk. And if the fire was not ablaze, then the chandelier of candles, which hung from the very middle of the room, shone down to give soft light to the sitting area just in front of the fireplace. The couches were mismatched but went together like a patchwork quilt. And in total, the room provided a comforting feel. It was an open and airy joint, which was on purpose, for sometimes, the mood in this place was anything but.

Today, if someone was peering into this quaint setting, they might mistake Annais for a cement statue. And his state of mind followed suit. It was heavy, and his mood might have very well weighed the room itself down. There was such gravity to his thoughts, it seemed they would manifest in a physical manner. In this frame of mind, Annais could be incredibly intimidating. With a stature of six foot, five inches, a stocky frame, and a few days of growth on his face, he looked a bit like a small bear or just a flat-out scary-looking man. When Annais was making critical decisions, his eyes took on a dark gray, like the gray in an old Detroit automotive plant: gray with a lot of brown and black mixed in, a worn-down, dirty gray. He sat back at his desk in the chair that had been custom-made for him. It was fashioned from cherry and black leather, the kind decorated with fancy brass tacks. It was the man's chair of all men's chairs. One large ominous cloud now stretched across all the windows at the west end of the office. Annais surmised this cloud had a couple good friends behind it.

Aha, he thought. *That's it.* He shook himself out of his own deep funk.

Good friends were exactly what he needed just now. He exhaled for what seemed like the first time in hours. He kicked his work boots up onto the desk (no one was there to tell him not to), placed his hands behind his neck, and looked back out to the darkening sky, this time with a plan in mind.

"Well, we might have to pull an all-nighter," he said out loud. "I wonder how the boys will take that."

If he could get his two most trusted advisors together, who also happened to be his best friends, he figured he might get through this predicament. A grin crept across his face for the first time in hours, and he half-chuckled. He could, in effect, force them to come here. But this had never been his style. And come to think of it, his friends always seemed to be of the same mind, anyhow. He picked up the black wall phone to call each of them. He could have just summoned them; it would have been faster. After all, he was in charge. And certainly, there were emergency situations that necessitated just that. In an emergency, it was his prerogative to boss people around. But this was not an emergency. Not yet.

By the time the other two arrived, Annais was pacing, and the rain was keeping step. It splattered against the wooden window frames and ran down in small rivers on the outside of each pane, illuminated by the quick flash of lightning every few minutes. When he heard their knock, he turned on his heels and greeted them at the door. Annais grabbed Asriel first. Asriel was a lanky, wiry man with a full head of white and silver hair and a distinguished beard to match. And then Xander, who was the opposite of Asriel: a stout fellow with wavy auburn hair and muscles that went on for miles. Others always commented on what a paradox it seemed that these two were Annais's best friends. But Annais reveled in being a contradiction to what others thought of him. And Xander and Asriel's presence always soothed his temperament instantly. He showed them how he felt with a bear hug and a kiss on the cheek.

Once everyone was inside, Annais strolled to a cabinet just next to his desk. He asked if Asriel and Xander would like coffee or a mulled, spiced tea. They exchanged knowing glances. This must mean it was going to be a long night. Not just a row over wine and a fire. Obviously disappointed, Asriel chose the tea and Xander the coffee. This was no surprise to Annais. He merely asked as a pleasantry. Resigned to their fate, Xander grabbed an armful of kindling and began to build a small fire, whilst Asriel went to Annais's desk and pulled out a few documents. Tattered and well worn, these were maps and assignment sheets. All three seemed to converge on the sofas at the same time. And with brevity, Annais skipped the niceties and delved right into the heart of the matter. As he spoke, the other two listened intently. If Annais's distinctly different friends had one thing in common, it was that they were both adept listeners who never missed a beat or a detail. They asked just the right questions at just the right time and communicated in such a harmonious fashion. They'd spent so much time as friends that it was effortless, really. Almost habitual. The minutest facial expression on one face spoke volumes to the other two. The honesty and transparency of their conversation made it akin to a beautiful dance of words and thoughts between the three.

The conversation was intense at times and filled with passion. Documents, names, places, events, and times flew around the room in a chaos which mirrored the wild weather outside. And then the meeting seemed to climax with the storm itself, culminating in a tremendous crack of thunder. When the thunder struck, Asriel and Xander both looked at Annais. And then a reprieve of silence slunk in, and a huge curtain of darkness seemed to lift. Over the room. Over the house. And over Annais. It wasn't long before the three of them were cracking jokes and throwing in a few innocent insults, one to the other. Finally, they grabbed each other in less tenuous bear hugs than the first. Hugs of gratitude. Sincere and strong. And then it was over. In a flash. Just like the storm. In and out and over. Annais stood with his hands in his pockets and a smile of relief across his face as he watched the other two walk down the tree-covered lane together. He missed them instantly, yet he knew they would rendezvous sooner rather than later. He took one last lingering look, spun on his heels, and made his way back to the fireplace. The fire was mostly embers now, but they could still warm his backside a bit. So he sidled up to it and turned about face.

He was now directly across the room from the painting above his desk. It was the only piece of art in the room and would have stolen the show even if it were not, as it measured six feet wide and four feet tall. Annais could often be found gazing at it. Those who were allowed in his office might not notice, as they were so infrequently there, but the piece was ever evolving. It might be taken for modern art, but had a large amount of Impressionist influence as well. The colors were brilliant, and it was bold. It portrayed many people who were all walking toward something. But the something was not in the frame. It was one of those pieces where a casual onlooker might interpret its meaning in a totally different manner than the artist intended. Annais was the artist, but he was happy to share the interpretation of it with anyone who was willing to look at it with him. He was more interested in sharing it than in telling others how to see it. This painting was a metaphorical representation of his time here in the Next Place. This was his lifelong work. And this work of art was a reminder to Annais. It was why he bled sweat and tears. And he wouldn't rest until it was perfect. And until it was finished. He knew it was coming. It would be a masterpiece. But it was still very much in the making.

As he gazed from across the room, his thoughts drifted back to his conversation with Asriel and Xander. And to the main subjects of the conversation: Tawly, Janey, and Abaddon. He had been advised to be patient. And to involve as few of the others as possible. This was difficult for Annais; he didn't like to sit idly by. Only he had met the likes of Abaddon. And only he could anticipate the evil of the Legion. It was like a game of chess to him. But this game had life-or-death consequences. He wanted to jump into the battle himself. But he knew his judgment was sometimes clouded by his passion, so he would take the advice of his two friends. They had yet to lead him astray.

"Yes," he said aloud to no one. "I will watch. And I will wait."

4

Tawly

Tawly approached Raynia slowly. She was almost hoping to sneak up on her. Something about Raynia was so mysterious, so ethereal, and it made Tawly want to seem sneaky. Sneaky was the closest she thought she could get to mysterious. Tawly couldn't quite put her finger on it, but back in the First Place, she knew she would have casually labeled Raynia as a free spirit. Now, as she walked up to her, she wondered what Raynia might have been named in the First Place: Moon Beam? Star? Jasmine? Or maybe something rather normal like Mellissa, Tawly mused. Whatever she had been called on earth, Raynia was a suitable name for her now. She had a sea green aura, which seemed to glimmer with a hint of gold. Underneath it all, she had a full head of brown hair that was kissed with golden highlights from her gardening. She usually had it all pulled up in a bandana, but tonight, it was down in her signature dreads. Apparently, Tawly was not all that sneaky, or else she was thinking too loudly, because Raynia had glanced over her shoulder at Tawly approaching. Her eyes were a deep brown and always seemed sort of settling to Tawly. Now, Tawly noticed something she had not before: Raynia not only had that comforting sea green aura and soothing stare, but she also seemed to be giving off a bit of heat.

Is that even possible? Tawly wondered.

As she pondered, she had the sensation of stepping into a warm bath on a cool spring evening. Tawly speculated that perhaps she had not really died in the hospital, but rather was just on some trippy drugs that had her in perpetual hallucination. This place was seriously crazy. People were heated? Raynia must have been watching Tawly closely because she looked at her keenly, raised her eyebrows, and opened her arms up as if to hug her. Tawly did a stutter-step, as she was unsure if people hugged here. Not for the first time, Tawly wished there was a manual for the Next Place: *The Next Place for Dummies*-type thing. Raynia answered by cutting the distance between them in half, and suddenly, Tawly was in the first embrace she could remember since she first arrived at the Next Place. That last hug (and the only one she could remember in her short weeks here) had come when she had met her Mender. In Raynia's arms, Tawly recalled how that had felt: to be mended. If she had anything to compare it to from the First Place, she decided it felt like watching her grandmother's eyes sparkle when she was explaining a life lesson to Iris or like lying on her daddy's shoulder and crying it all out when she was too sad to understand life.

Somehow, it also felt like the warm embrace of her mother when she got home from the first day of school. Perhaps it was like so many other safe and beautiful things all at once. Whatever it was, she had felt it in every cell of her body. And her mind had changed during that hug. That was all the Mender did. There had been no words. There had been no pomp or circumstance. It had merely been a hug. But in that one hug, it was as if every single hurt, betrayal, and disappointment had somehow been sucked up into the warmth of that embrace. The warmth. Yes, now Tawly remembered. It was a warmth. But like her heart was warming up. Like a slow burn. A good burn. She had felt like all the holes that had been carved into her soul by the First Place were slowly being rectified by something, like a thread that sewed an old stuffed animal back together. What the thread had been eluded Tawly. But it had left her feeling ecstatic. It seemed like it took forever, but at the same time, it was instantaneous. And when it had ended, the Mender had looked into Tawly's eyes. What Tawly had seen was her own reflection. But in an entirely different light than she had ever seen herself. A new Iris. For that was the only name she knew was hers. She had not been given her new name. That was to come later.

Tawly opened her eyes and stepped out of Raynia's embrace and the memory. Raynia held Tawly's shoulders and looked right into her eyes.

"What can I help you with?" Raynia asked, her stare boring directly into Tawly.

What was it about this place? Tawly thought. *People seemed to bypass the niceties and head straight for the heart of the matter. No detours. No chance to hide. Not even for a second.*

"What troubles you, fair Tawly?" Raynia offered.

And there it was: No beating around the bush. Apparently, there was no time for small talk in the Next Place. Tawly preceded to tell Raynia about how she had watched her daughter driving home from Walmart, how she had whispered to her in the left turn lane, how she had painted the sunset just to her Janey's liking, and how she had watched her retire to her home and little Gwin. Then she told Raynia that she figured Janey was safe for the night and had decided to come back to the Gathering Place. But just as she had left, she said she had sensed a strange presence. Raynia's eyebrows arched, and she seemed to anticipate the next sentence on the tip of Tawly's tongue.

"And how did you feel when you sensed this presence?" Raynia asked softly, almost hesitating.

"Dread" was the first word that came to Tawly. But then, she blurted out, "Confused, uncertain, out of control, angry, and panicked—all at once. But I have no idea about what."

"I see," Raynia said flatly.

The warm feeling Tawly had felt from Raynia seemed to be receding.

What in the world? she thought.

Raynia seemed to be sinking into a pensive place. She was withdrawing into her thoughts. She closed her eyes and was muttering. Or chanting.

Okay, this is not my cup of tea, thought Tawly. And just as she had resigned to about-face and leave, Raynia opened her eyes and stopped mumbling. She reached for Tawly's hand.

"Come sit for a second," she said as she led Tawly over to a table for two by the east windows.

Raynia sat down and stared at Tawly, who was starting to feel uncomfortable; she wished she hadn't asked Raynia anything.

"Someone is trying to kill Janey," Raynia said.

Tawly's gaze had wandered outside. Now she looked at Raynia. If she knew how, now she was looking right into Raynia's soul.

Who in the world is this quack I'm consulting with? Tawly wondered.

Tawly was clear that Janey was very depressed, that losing her husband and her mom in a two-week span had spun her into a cocoon of despair, and that Janey was floundering in the deepest funk Tawly had ever seen her in. And Tawly knew that it was her job to lift Janey's spirits and to get her back to her old self. But hunted? By a killer? Tawly found this preposterous.

Was this Raynia a complete loon? Tawly started to size her up and then scouted the room to see if there were any others around. Maybe she needed to make a quick ditch.

"Oh, Tawly," Raynia said in her singsong voice. "You think I mean someone else alive back on earth is trying to murder your daughter? No, no."

Oh boy, Tawly thought, holding her breath. *Here is where this wacko tells me she sees zombies.* She exhaled and said, "Well, yes, I would assume it was someone alive."

But Raynia just went on, "There are others, Tawly."

"Other whats?" Tawly shot back.

"Others like us," Raynia said.

Tawly mentally paused her escape plan and again looked into Raynia's eyes.

"Oh yeah?" Tawly taunted. "How so?"

Raynia could sense Tawly's distrust and unease. She spoke deliberately:

"They—the others—have passed from the First Place. But they chose not to come here to the Next Place."

"Well, where are they, then?" Tawly asked, incredulously.

This was making her more irritated by the second. Raynia seemed to be harboring some big secret, but she was taking her sweet time in telling it. And given Tawly now suspected Janey was in bigger danger than she once surmised, she wanted to reach across the table and shake the answer out of her.

Raynia shrugged her shoulders and said plainly: "Somewhere in between. There is an entire gang of them. They call themselves the Legion. And they are hunters."

Hunters? Tawly thought. All she could conjure up were guys in deer stands with beers, camo, and ammo, like her dad's buddies. On earth, Tawly's dad had bought all the hunting gear and could dress the part with the best of them. When deer season rolled around, he never seemed to head out hunting, though. Apparently, it was too far to drive before downing his beer. When the other guys headed out for deer hunting weekend, Tawly's dad had headed straight down the street to the local pub. He had gotten more attention, and his beers had come faster during hunting season, which he had happily capitalized on. The other guys had risked their lives shooting game with a bunch of other drunks, while he got drunker faster and with less distraction. If little Iris would ask him why he never came home with a deer, he would lie under the glare of her mom and say, "Maybe next time, sweetheart. Daddy's just a bad shot."

And the guys had always invited him over for venison, anyhow. They had all liked to show off their hunt. So he brought some other hunter's meat home to his sweet Iris, and she had forgiven him instantly. It had never mattered how drunk her father had gotten; when Iris was young, he had been her hero. As Tawly thought of her dad and his hunting buddies, she began to wonder about him now. Was he here in the Next Place? And could she see him somehow if he were?

But Raynia interrupted Tawly's memories of her dad with her next bombshell:

"No, Tawly; they hunt people, not animals. They hunt for life. And they seek to destroy it."

This was not at all the type of conversation Tawly had hoped to have.

"Oh. Okay. But ..." Tawly's voice trailed off.

She felt like she was shrinking.

"But why?" she asked meekly.

"You'd have to ask them that," Raynia replied.

Can people be smart alecks in the Next Place? Tawly thought. *Not likely,* she answered her own somewhat rhetorical question. She shook her head. The next obvious question surfaced and came out of Tawly's mouth:

"But why would they want to kill my sweet Janey?"

Raynia got a look on her face: a bewildered-mixed-with-crestfallen kind. She obviously did not have an answer.

"Sorry that I had to tell you," Raynia replied. "But after you described how you felt, I knew that a Destroyer must have been assigned to Janey."

Trembling, Tawly asked, "They are called Destroyers?"

It seemed to her that everything Raynia said brought another question and more dread.

Raynia said, "Yes, Destroyers."

But why? Tawly played with the question. It was always the whys with Tawly. Why this? Why that? She thought the Next Place was supposed to be full of answers. Not more questions. Now she grew irate.

"Tawly, I know what you are thinking," Raynia said. "Your answer is this: The Destroyers are out to crush anything which does not belong to them, that which they cannot have. In essence, this means they seek to eliminate anyone who exudes life, beauty, or purpose. And that is their purpose. Twisted. But true."

Tawly's heart sunk to the bottom of what felt like a bottomless well. The room started fading away. And for the first time in the Next Place, she felt what she had remembered as fear. And that made her even more afraid. She thought there was no fear here. Had she been tricked? This was her last waking thought, at least at the little table for two.

The next thing Tawly remembered was the sensation of being sweaty and groggy. Raynia must be super heating the joint, she thought as she started to come to. But as her eyes opened, she realized that Raynia was not here. In fact, she noted, she was dead alone. Under other circumstances, that might have sounded funny to her. Dead alone. She was indeed both. But it wasn't funny. Not tonight. It made her think of her Janey. And her chest felt heavy. She looked around. She was in the common area still, but now she was curled up on one of the bigger couches. And with her favorite afghan around her.

Ah, the afghan my grandma knit me," Tawly said to herself. *Now wait just a minute.* Tawly's eyebrows knit themselves together. "How could this be here?" She was talking aloud but to no one but herself.

She must have fallen off her chair at that little table with Raynia and hit her head. Maybe she had a concussion, which was clouding her thoughts. Clearly, things from the First Place could not make it to the Next Place. Tawly tried to remember her brief orientation to the Next Place. She had wanted to ask many questions, but she was told she would figure it out as she went. And she didn't recall anything specific about artifacts. But her afghan was here. It was her favorite. The one her grandma had let her help with when she was just seven. How could that be? She tried to recall: Had it been with her in the hospital? But that was not it. She knew it. Tawly could still remember the staunch ICU nurse who had insisted that even the lovely bouquet of fresh flowers, which was the last bit of livelihood in the room, had to go. She had given a dirty look to Iris's kids, grabbed the flowers, and marched right out into the hall and threw them in the trash. It had been such a nightmare to Iris: All those people just staring at her forlornly. All hoping but all knowing: Iris was going to die. And her

Janey had been the hardest to look at. Janey had looked like she had just seen a ghost. Empty eyes. Racing mind.

This memory made Tawly think of her Janey back on earth now, and she decided she needed to forget about the afghan. She would file that away and ask someone later. For now, she had to figure out how to get rid of Janey's Destroyer, whoever that was. So Tawly pressed her hand into the couch to raise herself up. The crinkling sound of paper caught her attention. There was a note, which had been lain next to her. Tawly realized this was only the second time she had gotten a handwritten note in the Next Place. It felt kind of thrilling, in a way. Her new name was written across the front, in the loveliest of penmanship. She opened it and read:

Sweet Tawly,

    I am sure you feel afraid.
    Rest assured, this is not the same kind of fear as you felt in the First Place.
    But it should spur you to action.
    As a Keeper, you are uniquely equipped to save Janey's life.
    Indeed, this is your current purpose.
    You have been perfectly prepared for just this.
    I promise you this. And a Mender's promise is unequivocal.
    If you have any other questions, seek Annais.

Well and kind of her, thought Tawly, *but I am certainly not seeking Annais.* Tawly had yet to meet the guy, but right now, she pictured him like the Wizard of Oz, like some little guy behind a big green curtain. If he were anything more, then these Destroyer freaks wouldn't be running around trying to kill people in the First Place. What a joke of a leader, she figured. Of course, there were all the things the others had to say about him. But Tawly was a "show me" kinda gal. This was a residue from her life in the First Place. She had been burned by enough folks to realize: You don't know them until you know them. Forget what people have to say. And so, for now, she forgot about Annais altogether. She could figure this out all by herself, she decided.

Tawly got up from the couch, grabbed her note from Raynia and her afghan from her grandma, and headed back to her room. It was comforting to have the afghan here. Even if it was a bit uncomfortable to not know how it got here. But for now, she would put that curiosity on the back burner, until she had the time and could ask someone. Tawly's list of questions was growing, as was her wonder. But it would all have to wait. She wanted to see her Janey first, just to know she was alive. And then she would make a plan. A plan to kill any chance of Janey's Destroyer killing her. She hated that they were called that. She could think of a few other choice names for them. But that wasn't her style. She had never been much of a name caller. By anyone's standards in the First Place, she was docile. And she had very rarely stuck up for herself. In the First Place, she had been the one who usually got walked all over.

"Not this time; not my Janey, not on my watch," she murmured under her breath as she walked briskly back to her room.

5

Jane

It was one of those mornings. The kind where little Gwin was teeming with life: hopping, laughing, singing, and generally pushing every button I had. Exuberance for life rubbed up against me in an altogether bristly fashion. Even if I was pleased that my own daughter was joyful, the presence of that joy stifled the manner by which I had learned to navigate each day. I had to avert it somehow. I was like the Grinch: I had to stop Christmas from coming.

"How about we go for a little adventure in the car?" I queried to an unsuspecting Gwin, who was currently wrestling the cat off the couch.

"Sure, Momma."

Her eyes lit up. I rationalized, she did not need to know that our big adventure would be a painstakingly slow circle from our town to the next. No purpose. No real adventure. Just the blatant wasting-away-of-time packaged surreptitiously into something I was doing valiantly for her. *I had turned into such a louse,* I thought to myself.

I headed into the kitchen and caught a glimpse of myself in the living room mirror. It stopped me short of the kitchen. I was worse than just a louse. I was a washed-up, good-for-nothing, good-for-nobody mess. I looked homeless (the irony being that most of the time, I was stuck in my home). My rosy complexion, which I inherited from my Irish and Norwegian grandparents, looked ashy. This was a fitting backdrop for my sullen expression. My hair, which had been pretty unruly my whole life anyhow, was now a disaster. Once my crowning glory, it now looked like a rat's nest. But that of a monster rat. I had too much hair for it to be a cute rat's nest. I momentarily wondered if I would scare people if they were to see me outside. Then I remembered: I could care less. I shrugged my shoulders at my reflection and started the preparation for a dead-on-arrival farce of an adventure.

I helped Gwin gather sojourners (stuffed animals, to be precise) and snacks. Then we struck out on our trek to Linden. It was exactly four miles from our safe house. Something about being in the driver's seat had always reduced my anxiety. It was almost meditative. Gwin was chattering in the back seat, and I was just entering that Zen-like mental, disappearing act when we rounded the corner into Linden.

"Momma?" Gwin peeped.

It was a clear departure from her ongoing dialog with her stuffed travelers.

"Yes, honey?" I said over my shoulder as I looked at her in the rearview mirror.

My voice was still weak, but was thickening into a honey sweet after these first few minutes of reprieve.

"Where is Mammie's stone?"

The question hung between the back seat and my right ear. Looming. I glanced out the windshield and realized we were passing the cemetery. A conversation we had shared months ago before my mom had died replayed in my mind. We had been passing this exact cemetery, and Gwin had wondered aloud, "What are all those big stones doing in that park?"

I had diligently explained that when someone leaves the earth, the people who loved them would make a stone for them. That way, they would have a place to go to when they wanted to think about that person whom they lost. Gwin had liked the idea of a stone and had told me, in her altogether too smart for a three-year-old way, that if she were to die, she would like for me and her daddy to pick her a "nice stone with puppies and ... kitties, yes both."

This had been the end of our conversation on that day. And I hardly wanted to pick it back up here with this new twist. It was the reality I was trying to escape with this drive. As if the many memories in this town were not reminder enough. Every building, every road, every store, every bump in the road— literally and figuratively— brought the memory of my mom coursing to life. And now, just as I was delivering myself, the actual stone which was supposed to be that place of remembrance had to surface. The decision to not have a burial site, to cremate my mom and spread her ashes, was just one sore spot in the myriad of battles we had fought as a family. And I certainly had not told Gwin about it. So her question remained: Where, indeed, was her grandmother's stone?

That day at the hospital actually started to paint itself back into my consciousness: The incredulous look on my sister's face when she came to me, armed with the news that our father had decided that they would cremate her body.

"How could he?" she had shot at me. "Did she really want that?"

How could I answer for sure? All of the implications had been swirling in my head and had produced that simultaneous gut-wrenching emptiness in the chest. I vividly remembered standing in the hallway of the ICU, staring back at my sister and having no idea how to answer nor how to make it all right. This memory inevitably fast-forwarded me to the next scene.

"I am going to spread your mother's ashes in places that were important to us," my father had declared.

And then on to the next horrifying memory: My dad had placed the cardboard box of ashes in the middle of the two bucket seats in the van. I would avert my eyes every time I got into the van, but I was wrestling with every other muscle in my body, which just wanted to look at my mom one more time. But my eyes could not take it. They had already seen what they had never thought they could bear to see.

The day after he had put the ashes in the van, I had borrowed it to go get my niece and nephew, and my niece had asked me, "Is Mammie really in that box?"

And I had barely been able to formulate a semblance of a response. My eyes had seen, but my heart did not believe.

And then, inevitably, the next memory would come: I couldn't keep my mind from revisiting that day at the funeral home. I had looked into the funeral director's eyes and asked, "Is my mom here?"

"Yes," he had said in a measured tone.

Just yes. That had been his response. I had not had any previous experience with cremation, but I had known that her body had to go somewhere before it happened. So then I knew. She had been in the basement of the funeral home. And I hadn't been able to figure out how that was okay. How was it okay for all of us to be up here alive and for her to be down there? But the director hadn't offered to let me go see her. I guessed that was not normal. And so, I had just sat there, staring at him. If I remembered correctly, we had stared at each other for a while.

Finally, the last and worst scene: Just a couple of days after that planning session, the day of the funeral arrived. I would never forget that day, as for five straight days to follow, my cell phone date had refused to change. And the date was the lock screen on the display. So for five days, every time I would look at my phone, I would see the date: October 11, 2010. And I could not deny it. My mom's funeral had happened. And I had planned it. On that day, when Gwin arrived all dressed up for what I had told her was "a party of sorts for Mammie," she had run around the funeral home, looking for her Mammie. It had been like hide-and-seek to her. In watching her, I had known I was playing a kind of hide-and-seek myself. I had wanted to hide from reality and to seek an escape from that very day. But it was my job as her mother. I had to tell her. I had to admit to her that her Mammie was not really there. Why hadn't I been able to just say the word: dead?

And now, as I looked into the rearview mirror and as we careened around the outskirts of the cemetery, I had to explain the absence of a gravestone. For Gwin's expectant eyes pierced through those decisions: mine, my dad's, my mom's, the family's. And there was no going back to fix anything. Our decisions were, ironically, set in stone.

I couldn't look at her, but I said it: "Your Mammie does not have a stone."

The next question was sure to come. Someday. But by some act of grace or mercy, she just stared back at me. Perhaps, she inherently knew that it was too much for me to bear. How could I possibly explain complex family dynamics, the weary history of lifelong relationships, and the kind of mixed-up things that happen to those in the company of grief? How the visit of death could rewrite what we once believed to be true. This was daunting to me and was certainly too much for a three-year-old. For now, it seemed clear to her; she would never have a place that she could "go" to remember her Mammie. For me, the opposite seemed true. I would never have a place that I could go where the memorial of her would not be there. Yet the stones I had were made not of cement but of places and scents and memories, of painting and dreaming together, of back roads travelled, of difficult moments endured, of living, and of dying, really. Monuments set in stone in the landscape of this world, a world where death always won. Or, at least, as far as I knew.

Tawly

If only she knew, Tawly thought as she gazed wistfully out the window. After her fainting spell at the lodge and the note of encouragement she had woken up to from Raynia, Tawly had marched back to her room with her old-new afghan and a newfound cup of ambition. She closed her eyes and wished herself right next to Janey's side. When she found herself back on earth, though, her daughter seemed to be on the move. Janey was putting stuff in her little sedan and was about to head out.

This is new, Tawly thought. *Maybe she is better off than I thought.*

Tawly had jumped right in the passenger seat. It was a pretty day for a ride, she figured. And she had been delighted as she realized that Janey was headed to Linden. Tawly had always loved Linden. It could have been a *Country Living Magazine* spread on small-town charm. And small-town charm? Tawly was all about that. Tawly, when she had been Iris, had seemed to invent charm itself when it came to decorating a home, and so she was delighted when the small town of Linden sprung up around her. She watched closely, and Janey seemed to calm down with each mile. Yet as soon as little Gwin mentioned her Mammie, Janey seemed to ricochet back to her half-stupor. As Tawly rode along and watched the most recent drama unfold in Janey's experience of her death, she wished that Janey could instead see the landscape of what was around her. Not for the hurt of the past but for the beauty of the present.

If only she could be privy to what was to come, Tawly thought. *Then, perhaps, her outlook would be through rosier glasses.*

But how could she ever open Janey's eyes? She certainly couldn't sneak her into the Next Place. And how could she make her strong enough to face a Destroyer? Right now, Janey was like one of the Three Little Pigs: the one in the straw house, to be precise. It wouldn't take much effort on the Destroyer's part to blow her house right down, Tawly estimated. She looked over at Janey now. She was pained by her blank look and crushed spirit. She knew that Janey was having a hard time with the reality that she was gone. And the whole back and forth with little Gwin about her stone (or lack thereof). The gravitas of it seemed silly to Tawly. It was just a stupid stone. But of course, she had the advantage of knowing what she knew now. The worst part of it all to Tawly was that she was watching her daughter, who had always seemed to have a purpose and direction, drive around in pointless circles, going nowhere.

Tawly wracked her brain as Janey turned the radio back up, and Gwin went back to her stuffed animal circus. She briefly considered seeking out Annais. But then she rejected that thought. Instead, she would return to the Gathering Place and find someone else to help her. But first, she would see that Janey and Gwin got into their little house.

She would make sure she didn't have any eerie feelings, and then she would return to her cozy little lodge.

The rest of the car trip proved uneventful. Gwin sang. Janey brooded. Janey did drive through the Tim Horton's for a coffee and a sprinkle donut for Gwin on the way back through town. But the donut shop was as adventurous as it got. Janey pulled back into their driveway, unloading little Gwin without a word, and they both got out and went back into their quiet house. The smell of Tim Horton's gave Tawly a hankering for some good, fresh java back home. It was funny; she thought of it as home now, she reflected. She thought to check inside Janey's house first, to be sure everything appeared normal. She peered in through the little window in the front door. She could have just as easily gotten herself inside, but she still felt a little odd about lurking around the house. So she just scanned the joint. Everything seemed just so. Janey had turned the Sprout channel on for little Gwin and was in the kitchen, cooking up some macaroni and cheese. Tawly felt the heaviness of the household, even outside. But at least they were safe, she surmised.

So she turned to go. As she did, she noticed the mailbox. She didn't know why, but she decided to snoop inside. What she found was at least a month's worth of mail. And the good majority of the envelopes were bills. Bills with Janey's name on them. Bills with her ex-husband's name on them. Letters from the city, from the court, from the bank, and from her last employer. It would seem Janey just did not care about any of it. This was nothing like the Janey she had raised and known. She seemed to have lost herself completely in the couple months, since Iris had died. But how in the world could she get Janey to recognize that? She would be under water financially soon, and then she might die of the stress alone. Never mind the grief and the despair. Tawly took one last look around, placed the mail back in the box, closed her eyes, and reluctantly returned to the lodge.

6

Jane

I awoke on my stomach, face in the pillow, with a start. No, make
that an acute awareness: Someone was calling me out of bed. I was
entangled in my mom's shawl and raised my head up just enough
from the bed to look out the small window. Yet I knew that what was
beckoning me was not outside at all. It was in the room. Behind me.
In the corner. This would necessitate me doing a full turn in bed. It
felt like another person calling to me. *No,* I thought. *Now, wait just a
second.*

I stopped myself. It was the middle of the night. I was in bed,
alone. There were no cries from Gwin's room, which was just across
the hall. The dogs were not pacing nor whining. The house itself was
completely silent: an absolute lack of any sound whatsoever. But even
in this vacuum of sound, I could now hear clearly: "I am here. Turn.
Rise up. Come with me."

This time, I had no second thoughts. The command was
consuming. I now felt no choice or any cause for alarm. The ease of
heeding the call contrasted sharply with my disheveled attempt to get
out of the covers, to untangle from my mom's chemo shawl, and to
uncoil from my every-which-way pajamas. On my feet finally, I looked
down and saw my socks. Half-on and half-off. *Must be a mirror to my
brain,* I thought. And then I felt that presence again. I noticed that a

night light was glowing in the corner. But was it glowing more keenly than usual? What was this? I felt like I was being summoned. But I was in the bedroom of my house in the middle of the night, and there was nowhere to go. *Just walk to the kitchen*, I heard—without hearing.

Okay, sure. Maybe I can down some Advil PM and the last of that bottle of wine, I reasoned to myself. That should put me back to sleep. Maybe the wine is summoning me? When I arrived at the kitchen, to my disappointment, there was only a ring of the Riesling I preferred in the bottom of the bottle. And the Advil was about out, as well. Probably not best to mix them, anyhow. I flipped the light on in the dim kitchen. Offended by the light and the lack of anyone who had called me out to the kitchen, I closed my eyes, took a deep breath, and told myself I had every reason to be a little off-kilter these days. I chalked it up to midnight madness and purposed my way back toward the bedroom. Two steps past the computer desk, almost to the bedroom, the calling returned: "Go back."

"To the computer?" I asked, incredulously.

Now, this must be a joke. I despised my computer. Even though it had afforded me a living for many years, I had allowed it to collect dust these past few weeks—or was it months? It was probably sitting on some lost asset list right now and would most likely remain there because ... Who was I kidding, anyhow? I would never work again in this condition. I was doomed to roam the halls of my house late at night in a wide-eyed stare, listening to voices that were not there. This would continue while Gwin's life went on around me. Until I died. Perhaps a little dramatic, but the last thing I wanted to do was to get back on that computer. I turned defiantly back toward the bedroom and then lost the argument. I shuffled around the coffee table, plunking down on the couch, and after the beast booted up, I opened up my Hotmail. I did the one thing I could stand to do anymore: Delete e-mails. I deleted them without care and with abandon. This was not at all like me. I deleted e-mails from old high school friends, from old co-workers, from bill collectors, from lawyers, from real estate agents, from my mom's best friends; those were the most excruciating to look at. I couldn't help the thought: Why were they still alive and not her? Delete. Delete. Delete. Sigh. Release. Guilt. Deleting these people's attempts at compassion would not get to the heart of the matter. But when you are at rock bottom, you will buy into any rock-shod attempt at denial. This was mine. In my hasty delete-fest, an e-mail from my mom accidentally ended up on the bottom of Page 1. I had gone back too far. An emotional panic attack began. I flipped randomly to one of my other folders. Ah, the Junk mail. Here, I could lose myself entirely. I could get totally caught up in "sleaze and breeze": my favorite label for the absolute nonsense that permeates our online experiences. It was all so stupid, weightless, invaluable. I could go on and on in a litany of hatred that did not land on any one person; somehow, this was an outlet for my rage. Until I saw one message with a strange address and an intriguing subject line. What SPAM would request fifteen minutes of my time for an interview based on a colleague's recommendation? Hmmm. I decided to open this one. It was from a recruiter. The phrases jumped out as I skimmed for the crux of the e-mail:

Speaking to someone nonchalantly in the break room ... Amazing opportunity ... working from home ... perfect candidate ... they thought of you ... not sure where you are or what you are doing currently ...

Well, if they only knew where I was right now. And what I was doing. Perhaps they would recant. A possible notion of this working out for me and Gwin surfaced. Bobbed around. And then I allowed it to float away. But I moved the e-mail to my inbox, just in case I would ever be employed again. I took note that I now felt a grogginess and fog setting in. I powered down, looked around, and realized that the calling had stopped ... if it had ever happened anyhow. I gladly got up and took myself back to bed. And although I did not stop to contemplate it, I did see on the way back to the bed that the night light was a tad dimmer now.

Tawly

Tawly watched Janey go back to bed. How many times she had watched this same scene as Janey had grown up. Only then, it had been from the vantage point of the living. Tawly stopped to recall the very first time baby Janey had slept in her own room. She had been four years old at the time. As a mother, Iris had loved to accompany her kids to their bed and read them to sleep. It was so soothing to her that she often fell asleep right next to them. She had decided to rein herself in on this occasion, though. She had wanted her Janey to find her own way. And letting her put herself to bed was one way she could let her daughter do that. As Janey grew, the ways in which Iris would let go of her would grow, as well. But on that night, she had simply let her walk to her own bedroom, alone. This would be the first time that little Janey had to stare down the darkness herself. She would need to calm herself all by herself. Odd, Tawly thought now as she watched Janey clamber back into bed: She had taught Little Janey how to face down the darkness of her bedroom back then. And now she had to teach her how to battle darkness on a much larger scale.

Tawly once again marveled at the ability to remember everything that had happened during her life on earth and how it intermingled with everything she felt and understood now in the Next Place. Yesterday, when she had noticed all the bills and all the stress that must be piling up on her daughter, Tawly recalled something crucial about her Janey's personality, something which seemed totally absent now: independence. Janey had always worked and taken care of herself. Ever since college, Janey had been able to support herself. And now, she was not only not working, she was without a husband, as well. And she was taking care of a three-year-old. How would she ever make it? Tawly knew that Janey had quit her job a few days after the funeral, assumedly because she couldn't figure out how to leave the house most of the time. But still, Tawly figured if she could find her a new and enticing job, then perhaps Janey could find a little motivation and subsequent hope on her own.

When this epiphany had hit Tawly, she was so excited that she went straight to the common room of the lodge. She saw one person over by the fire. She seemed to be dusting the mantle of the fireplace. *Were there Cleaners here?* Tawly thought. Not likely, but maybe they all had chores? Had Tawly been skipping her chores and not realizing it? Was she supposed to be doing dishes? It had all seemed to happen magically, she quipped back to herself. But before she could get on in her head with the rest of the argument, the other person stopped dusting and turned to Tawly. She had overheard Tawly's thoughts.

She looked at her and said sweetly, "No, I am another Keeper. I'm just in between assignments. And I rather like to clean house."

"Well, you don't find that every day," Tawly said with a smile.

This was a timely encounter. Another Keeper would surely know how to help Tawly. She had one burning question, and she got right to it:

"I need your help. I have to know. How do I make people on earth do things I want them to do?"

Well, it turned out that this was much easier than Tawly had imagined. The only trick was, you could not make them do something; you could only inspire them.

"You simply whisper in their ear," the other Keeper had explained. "And they hear it in their head. But what they chose to do with your suggestion, well, that is entirely up to them."

Tawly thought that sounded easy. Her next question was perhaps a more perplexing one:

"Then how do I find a job for my daughter? A certain job? Not just any job will do."

The other Keeper looked at Tawly and said, with what she thought was a touch of disdain:

"Did you consider the Resource Room?"

"No. What is that, exactly?" Tawly asked.

Realizing that she was ignorant, and apparently glad to be able to enlighten her so she could get back to cleaning, the other Keeper led Tawly to a door just off the coffee room. Tawly had noticed it before but had always thought it was a pantry door. When the door opened, Tawly was reminded of a Michigan basement. It felt like a cellar.

She hesitated and looked at the other Keeper, who said, "Don't worry. Once you get down there, it will all make sense."

So Tawly ventured down the steps. As she descended, she started to imagine what might be around the corner once she got to the bottom. She thought of the technology and robots in science fiction movies. She imagined a mission-control-type setting from the *Apollo 11* movie. It must be wicked cool, she figured. It was, after all, the Resource Room of the Next Place. But when Tawly rounded the corner, all she found was a peculiar-looking individual at a desk with a green lawyer lamp, shining like a beacon in the otherwise dark room.

"Oh, excuse me," Tawly said. "I must have taken a wrong turn."

"Certainly not," the funny-looking man said.

Tawly noticed some strange light around him, and she wondered how he would know if she had taken a wrong turn or not.

"Because I know everything," the man replied.

He looked up from his writing and set down his pen.

"I find that hard to believe," Tawly said curtly.

It was the show-me side of her coming out.

"Try me," the man said, almost playfully.

Tawly knew she had him. She smirked and retorted, "Okay, why am I here, then?"

"To save your daughter," the man replied with a straight face.

"Too easy," Tawly said, although she was slightly impressed.

"You are looking to help her get back to work," the man then said. "And I am here to help you with just that. My name is Cato. And I am a savant of sorts."

Tawly was surprised again. But she didn't have the time to argue. She was learning to just trust that what she knew for sure in the Next Place was that she didn't know everything. And she would need to just learn as she went. She vaguely remembered someone telling her just that. So she walked over to Cato's desk and sat down in the chair opposite him. He pushed his piece of paper across the desk to her, and she realized that it was a list he had been making: a list of possible jobs for her Janey. She looked up at Cato with growing affection.

The hardest part turned out to be sorting out what she thought would work for Janey. What might she be able to handle, given that Gwin was still little? Cato seemed to know everything, but he deferred to Tawly when it came to making the final decision. After all, Tawly knew Janey best. Tawly reflected that interacting with Cato was kind of like talking to one of those search engines back on earth: Siri or Alexa. But Cato not only spewed out possibilities, he also proffered a bit of wisdom along with it. As tentative as she had felt upon arriving in the basement, she now felt like she and Cato were old friends. They studied the possibilities earnestly. After much debate, Cato and Tawly had decided on one job.

Cato had found a company called SourceCloud and a nice remote position which Janey was perfectly qualified for. He gave her the location of the company's headquarters, the names of the two recruiters she should find (Doug and Ron), what times they typically took breaks, and how to get to the room they took breaks in.

So a few minutes later, Tawly had found herself in the breakroom of SourceCloud, where she whispered Janey's name in Doug's ear. Doug was talking to Ron. Ron had been looking to fill this position for close to a year now. He worried people were starting to doubt his recruiting savvy. This was just as Cato had told her. She wondered how this would all play out. But apparently, Cato had done his homework. Doug had interviewed Janey for a different job about a year ago. And he had never thought of her for the job Ron was trying to fill. Until now. Until he heard her name in his head. Tawly watched as the recruiter seemed to hear her and then got a grin on his face. The kind you get when you have a grand idea. And then, to Tawly's delight, he mentioned Janey to Ron and said she would be perfect for the vacant position. Doug looked up her contact information in his old e-mails and handed it over. Sure enough, Ron thanked him and headed straight back to his desk. With Janey's contact info in hand, he had sat down to pen her an e-mail.

Tawly felt satisfied that she had been able to arrange this. All she had to do next was to make sure Janey read the e-mail. But now that she knew how to whisper into someone's ear, she had figured it would be easy. The prospect of a new job was something she really thought Janey might look forward to. Tawly had found a new sense of determination: She was going to build up her daughter's arsenal against the Legion. She just hoped it would be enough. And soon enough.

7

Jane

I awoke a bit groggy, thanks to my midnight rendezvous with the computer. Some hideous noise had jarred me, as if someone was breaking into the house. I listened more closely. Ah, no; it was just my father, I told myself. Ugh. I hated it when I had to get out of bed. But to have a witness to my just-got-out-of-bed head and the gloomy look I seemed to ring each day in with added insult to my injury. My dad wasn't the most pleasant of alarms, either. He had this brash way of pounding on the door like something was on fire and then just barging in.

I ambled out, averted eye contact, and made a futile attempt at a welcome. Before I could even be really rotten, though, he had coerced me into waking, dressing, and feeding a half-asleep Gwin. He announced they were going to the Detroit Zoo.

"Splendid," I muttered.

He might have said Timbuktu. What did I care? Once he and Gwin had left, I stood staring at the door they had closed behind them for who knows how long. I then did a 180, shot an ugly look at my computer as I walked by, and went directly back to bed.

I spent the latter half of the day meandering back and forth, from the fridge to the window and the window back to the fridge, never really eating and never really seeing anything. Just kind of a slow waltz of waste, a way to pass the dull hours of wakefulness. At some point during the afternoon, my dad called to let me know they were home from the zoo and back at his house. I stewed over the fact that he had not brought her back to my place, but how much could I really ask of him? So I got all my energy up to go retrieve Gwin from his house.

One task at a time, I assured myself.

I began by pulling my unbrushed hair into a pony tail. Then I made an attempt at removing the prior day's mascara from underneath my puffy and blank eyes. And finally, I forced myself into a clean set of clothes. It was 5:30; it seemed a bit unnecessary to change now. But my father would be worried if I came in my pajamas. And so, I muddled through. I thought to check my appearance in the mirror. But even a quick look into the mirror was difficult. Seeing myself materially meant I had to accept that I was still stuck on earth. And then I had to admit I would rather be dead. It was too disheartening. So I turned away from the bathroom mirror, put the dogs in the study room, and walked out the door, to my own chagrin. There was a minuscule reward in all of this Herculean effort; I felt a tad victorious when I closed the door behind me. It was like a mini celebration that I could still function like a human.

Upon arriving at my dad's, though, the slight mood lift was dampened instantaneously. I looked at Gwin. She seemed happy enough. She had a stuffed gorilla under one arm and half a bag of cotton candy under the other. She ran up to me with her cute half-sentences spilling out. But apparently, the zoo and all its frivolities didn't work the same magic on my dad. He was in a dour mood and completely out of sorts. No doubt, I thought somberly, it must be the impending day. My mom's birthday was tomorrow. It might have been what had inspired him to take Gwin to the zoo.

March 21 had always been such a hopeful time of the year for a birthday. Spring in Michigan brought about a resurrection of nature. And Iris just loved nature. Her birthday itself used to bring a day of smiles upon Iris's face, which altogether might have lit up the whole world. But now, it seemed to be bringing a strange uneasiness for those she left behind. Uncertainty as to what to do. Stabs in the dark at planning to make cakes or buy flowers. Feelings of idiocy for planning to celebrate someone who was dead. These thoughts were interspersed with a kind of high for having every right to spend all day long thinking about her. Who could argue with us? But, to be honest, no one outside the family really cared about the day, anyhow. Just thinking about it put me back in a funk, and I decided that this was what my dad's foul mood must have stemmed from. I didn't want to abandon him on this night. So to avoid running out the door on my dad in his birthday-eve-groveling, I asked Gwin if she wanted to stay for a bit. She squealed. I took that as a yes. Perhaps my melancholy would somehow mix with his dour, and we could have less than a horrible night altogether, I considered.

Instead, it went from bad to worse. There was little I could say or do that was not perceived as an attack or some sort of ill-directed scheme. And so, as the night bore on, I figured a walk would do me and my dad some good. I eased out the front door while Gwin colored rainbows in the corner under the lamp and his watchful eye. The glow of the TV and my dad melded together as I escaped gingerly down the porch stairs. Walking very softly gave me the illusion of not really being physically present. If I wasn't present in this place, then maybe it would not hurt so much, I theorized. I walked as if I were just an observer of the world. There was a stripe of stars above me, between the trees on my mom and dad's street. I had to call it that still. If it were only my dad's street, would she have ever been there? A little house on the left gave call to notice. I had not seen it before. How could that be? I puzzled. Mom and dad had lived here for over ten years. Kind of sweet and kind of run-down, I thought. An older lady? Maybe dad could help with her lawn? Which is what I noticed next. There were pine trees in this lawn. Were there even pine trees in this neighborhood? And there was a clothesline. And wait, what was that?

There was movement. Enough to stop my own feet. It was the sound of rushing wind. It was loud enough to catch my attention but soft enough not to startle me. As I listened, I noticed something musical about it. It was almost melodic, I mused. It gave me a comforting feeling. Like a stanza from an old favorite song that comes on the radio. Or perhaps the sound of your backyard chimes, which after years carry a tune embossed on your heart's memory. It just felt so familiar.

What was it?

I felt certain that someone must be hiding under the shelter of those trees, playing some sort of musical instrument. My eyes bore into the entwined pine trees that I would have sworn were newly planted today. I peered around and felt the irresponsible urge to run in to those trees.

Get yourself together, Jane, I scolded myself. *The neighbor, whoever she is, will call the police. She? Why did I think it was a lady? Ugh, this was ridiculous.*

I turned my head, picked up my foot, and decided to walk loudly on. Just in case someone was really in the bushes, thinking I was an easy target for ambush; I would show them just how strong I was. But before my foot even made contact, a whispered version of my childhood lullaby arrived on the cool night breeze, reaching my ear: "I love you a bushel and a peck ..." The voice was so soft, but I heard it over the wind. My senses froze. The understanding, the intuition, and the knowing came all at once. And through the dark between us, I wanted to call out:

"Momma, is that you?"

Tawly

Tawly had been watching Jane. She had wanted to see if the new job prospect had changed her disposition at all. Plus, it was protocol. On the days leading up to a birthday or a holiday, a Keeper was to pay very close attention to the Loser. This was a mandate on the Keeper. Losers must be blanketed with attention. So Tawly had arrived early in the morning and stayed with Janey all day. She was a tad disappointed in how Janey had spent the first part of her day: meandering around her living room. Before Tawly died, she has always likened her Janey to a Mexican jumping bean: always bouncing out the door from one thing to another, barely taking a minute to breathe. Tawly knew that this earthly birthday was important to Janey, but she also knew there were additional dates once you got to the Next Place, and there would be celebrations so set apart from cakes and candles, so astounding in comparison that if Janey had any idea what kind of parties her mom was going to go to ... well, she would not be worried in the least about tomorrow.

Of course, Janey could not know for now. Tawly understood this. For tonight, Tawly must shield her. And so, she had decided to wait down the street while Janey was at her dad's ... and to escort her and Gwin home when they left. To her delight, though, her daughter had appeared on the street, walking with care and a concerned look on her face. Tawly was allowed to bring comfort to Jane's soul in many ways, but revealing herself here on earth and speaking out loud was out of the question. She did not even have that power. That was strictly for Annais, at his own time and according to his own call. So as Jane approached the part of the street where Tawly was hiding, she decided on something she was allowed to do. She sang an old lullaby that she had soothed Jane to sleep with thousands of times:

I love you, a bushel and a peck;
a bushel and a peck and a hug around the neck;
a hug around the neck, about you.

She sang with the voice of the Next Place, which on earth manifested in the sounds of nature. But somehow, Janey heard more than the wind. And Tawly knew she did. She saw Janey stop and look over at where she was hiding. Tawly was afraid Janey might just run right into the pine trees. It felt like when you were little and playing hide-and-go-seek at dusk, and you were so scared in your hiding that you just wanted to be found. But for the rules, you would have run right out to the seeker and crushed them in a "You found me!" hug. Tawly wanted exactly this. To run right out and give herself up. Of course, this could not happen now. You could not show yourself to your Loser. It was in the rules. And Tawly was just not a rule breaker. She wished she was at that very moment, though. She was considering what it would be like to embrace her sweet daughter. To feel the warmth of her heart.

And then Tawly saw what she had not seen yet: a Destroyer. If she had not glanced at the stars that shone down on her lovely daughter, who looked a little stunned and a little ecstatic, she would not have noticed him on the roof. He was one house behind. And he was calculating. Tawly feared he was going to jump right on top of Jane. She had never seen who the Legion had sent for Jane, but she knew from whence he came at first glance. That same ominous feeling, like the night she escorted Janey home from Walmart, cloaked Tawly now.

Raynia had told her, "You will know them when you see them. It is just something they give off."

Tawly could see ambition, motivation, and pride on this figure as obviously as a person on earth could see color. These things oozed out of the man on the roof. In the dark of the night, they appeared as embers which he dusted off his coat as he sat in contemplation. Tawly focused on his face. He had not glanced her way. He must have not sensed her yet. She saw the determination in this creep's heart to destroy Janey. She saw it, and she remembered it all at once. But how could that be? She panicked as she tried to figure it out. She could hear the insults he was spewing out to try and consume Jane's thoughts. Some of this sounded so familiar. Could he be affecting Tawly's mind too? No. She knew that once her soul had been mended, it was immune from such nonsense. Then why could she hear it? And then it dawned on her.

This guy had been sent for her on earth as well. In her forties, when she was on the brink, he had come to finish her off. He had spoken similar things. Tawly was becoming unnerved. How could this be? She had almost given up her very life due to this creep's lies. And now? She had to battle him for her own daughter's life? She wanted to wring his neck right there. But that, of course, was not a way in which this guy could be defeated. She had been told that Destroyers would eventually die from their own heart's deterioration. But to defeat him in this battle, for now, she must only keep her Janey alive. She glanced over at Janey and saw her shake her head, probably hearing from the Destroyer that she was just delusional, that the beautiful music she was hearing was only her imagination.

"Just face it, Jane. Your mom is gone, and you should go too," the vulgar voice spewed.

Tawly could hear bits and pieces of his ugly voice, as she tried to put it all together. But when she had sung to her daughter, she could see the effect that had on her. The lullaby had spoken some hope to Janey's heart; Tawly knew that was a small victory, even if the Destroyer was already causing her mind to argue with her heart. On earth, people did not perceive it, but something deposited in your heart was exponentially more powerful than your thoughts. Acts of love spoke to the soul and could cover a lifetime of lies spoken to the mind. This was a clear advantage for the Keepers. The Legion and its kind, even the seasoned ones, did not comprehend this.

Jane had been so jarred by the song and Abaddon's subsequent onslaught that she had forgotten about the rest of her walk and had turned around to head back to the house. The Destroyer took one more shot at her and Tawly could hear each word.

"You are a burden on your family, Jane. You cannot get along with your father anymore. You are an absent mother, who will only make Gwin's life worse. And you could not even make your marriage work. Why on earth do you think you are needed here? You are *not*."

This last sentence stopped Janey and Tawly both. Tawly looked at the Destroyer and then back to take stock of Janey; she was looking blankly ahead into the darkness, like she did not know where or who she was. She wasn't moving at all. She was just standing in the middle of the dark road. All alone. The Destroyer was grinning, like a fighter who had just won round one, decisively.

He jumped down and strolled over to the window of Tawly's old house. Tawly saw him look down at Gwin, who was still coloring innocently in the corner. He was trying to speak ill words over Gwin, just for a quick thrill. But Tawly saw the venom bounce back to him. There was a protection on the young ones. This was another thing the Legion just did not understand. And so, in his ignorance, the Destroyer shrugged his shoulders, shot a menacing look at Tawly's husband and granddaughter, and walked casually away into the dark of the night.

This threw Tawly into a tailspin. She watched until Janey eventually lumbered back into the house. And then without another thought, she returned to the Gathering Place and started looking for Raynia. What she found was not what she was hoping for. The lodge was uncannily empty, and there beside a blazing fire was the strange Taker she had seen several days ago. She noted now that he carried a rosy red aura. And fittingly, he looked like he had been through a firestorm tonight.

Ugh, she thought. *There must be someone else to talk to.*

Before she could turn to look somewhere else, though, her eyes were drawn to the fireplace. It was burning a magnificent white color. Tawly was unaware how long she gazed at the fire. But when she looked up, the Taker had crossed the room and was standing next to her, with his head cocked to one side.

"I am Twyjan," he said. "So very pleased to meet you."

He must be one of those who perceives everything, Tawly thought.

"Yes, I am," he said, smiling.

She returned his sweet smile. She thought to ask him why the fire was burning white. But she reasoned there would be a better time for that and opted to get down to business:

"My name is Tawly, and I need your help."

Tawly recounted the scene she had come from: the Destroyer hunting her daughter, Tawly realizing he was the one who had hunted her when she was on earth as Iris, him trying to affect her granddaughter, Gwin. Twyjan listened intently. He did not miss a spoken syllable or an unspoken emotion. When Tawly finished, he embraced her. She felt his strength and was comforted by that.

But then he said something which jarred her: "You must call on Annais."

This rubbed her the wrong way. She was kind of tired of everyone telling her to go see Annais.

"Don't you remember your arrival?" Twyjan queried. "You were given some guidelines. And that was one of them. If there are questions, seek Annais first."

Well, Tawly recalled this. But after everything she had learned about Annais, he was like the top dog around here. Would he really care so much about her dilemma?

"Oh yes, he cares about everything that you, I, and everyone else is facing," Twyjan said with sincerity.

Tawly knew that in this place, there was no chance you were being fooled, but this she found to be foolish, indeed. Twyjan knew Tawly needed to move on her own now. He winked at her, squeezing her hand. And then he was up and was headed for the coffeemaker.

Jane

I opened one eye. The daylight that crept in was way too much. I had to close it. I tried to back up, to fall back into the bliss of sleep. Not likely today. The date had already emblazoned itself across my consciousness. The idea of a party came to mind. How cruel. There would be no party. No one would get together. I had even resolved not to contact any of the family. It felt like a poor attempt at feeling sorry for myself. Why celebrate her birthday, when that only led to her eventual departure? I was on fire mad already, and I had only been up for a hundred seconds. Anger: It chewed around every other emotion I might experience these days. Even when looking at my sweet little Gwin in her most ecstatic state—say, running through the sprinkler—there was an enemy line of bitterness and toil that was always making its move. Hunted; I always felt hunted. On occasion, it actually felt as if there were bodies out there. Like the presence of darkness itself. Thieves that were lurking just out of sight. I could not imagine what they might want from me though. Everything had been taken. Except Gwin, of course.

No, I told myself. *They would not take Gwin. Of course, not Gwin.*

I would take out Death itself if it tried to take my Gwin. And then, truth be told, if I lost, I would just give it up, anyhow. She was my last lifeline. The irony did occur to me. Today was my mom's birthday. And without her, I would not be here. And without me, Gwin would not be here. But without Gwin, I would not be here either. How was it that I had needed both of them to survive? First, my dear mom ushered me into this life, then she spent many years sheltering me from it, and then I would lean on Gwin to be anchored to it. Lest I let go. What a twisted plot. I might just stay in bed for the rest of the day and ponder the wicked puzzle my life had broken into.

But alas, it was 7 a.m., and Gwin was like clockwork.

"Mommmmaaaaaa!" she called out to me.

She knew the instant she awoke, whether I was in bed with her or not. This time, I was not. I had suffered during the drive home from my dad's the night before. The voice had been relentless. It had kept repeating in my mind:

You are not necessary. You are not necessary. You are not necessary.

I had believed it. I had no reason not to. I had just wanted to get to bed so it would quit. My only safe place was sleep. Gwin had fallen right to sleep. And I had wanted to wake up on my mom's birthday wrapped in her shawl. One more attempt to continue the shelter-charade.

So now, I disentangled myself from the woolen security blanket, found my way across the hall in the pre-dawn darkness, and tiptoed into my little one's room.

"Momma?" she whispered in the dark. "Is that you?"

My heart folded over itself as I remembered the evening past.

8

Annais

Tawly had been summoned, as it were, the moment she inquired how to reach Annais to ask him her all-consuming question. She had arrived at a large wooden door. Intuitively, she had knocked. And the door swung open to reveal an older gentleman. He had a full head of salt-and-pepper gray hair and was donning an outdoorsman-type outfit. She might have guessed it was the groundskeeper. Yet, even though he hadn't said a word to her, she knew this was Annais. Perhaps there was a Cabela's here, she kidded to herself. Or maybe Annais ordered from the Sundance catalog. Amused with herself, and hoping he couldn't hear her thoughts like everyone else here, Tawly offered a quick smile to Annais. He raised his eyebrows and grinned right back.

"I've been expecting you," he said warmly.

"Figures," she mumbled under her breath.

Annais seemed unfazed and motioned for her to come in. She stepped over the threshold into what she had thought was a home. He was holding the door in his right hand and had his left hand in his pocket. He was acting rather casual, she noticed. But she didn't have much time to judge as she then saw him free up his hands and cut the distance between them to embrace her in his grasp, which proved to be suffocating and comforting at the same time. Her fear dissipated out the doorway behind her. He hadn't said a word, just the hug. Tawly noticed a strong scent of cedar and sage. It made her feel high in some manner. Now, as she looked up at him, her question seemed so little. The very stature of Annais made her jaw drop a bit. She backed out of his embrace.

He turned and began walking with purpose. A bold confidence whisked in behind her as she walked behind Annais, though she knew not why. A few steps in, she changed her mind. It must not be a home. The room that the entryway opened into felt more like a barn. And the farther they walked, the more it felt less like a building and more like the outdoors.

No, wait, she thought. *This is a tent made out of trees.* There were many very tall trees surrounding them now, and the tree branches created a long, narrow tunnel. They were walking on a dirt path, and it was so very pretty that Tawly started to fall behind. It was akin to driving the roads in up north Michigan at the height of Indian summer. It was lit, softly. The leaves of the trees displaced the afternoon sun, which shone in just enough to create an orange glowing effect. It was warm and inviting, and bird songs aggregated into a cacophony of a sound track. Tawly heard a few leaves crackle as they busted up under Annais's deft yet heavy footsteps. This made her look up; she quickened her gait when she realized he was several paces ahead.

Tawly felt like she was with her grandfather, her father, her husband, and someone else she could not put her finger on, all at once. She was still trying to grasp why this was when Annais led her off the path and into a clearing. It was bit brighter here, with fewer trees. He led her to a picnic table under a lovely old oak tree and asked her to sit down. She sat down and then watched as he lowered himself to the bench seat across from her. She had not noticed before, but in this light, she could distinguish that Annais had an aura around him too, just like everyone else here. But she could not describe what color it was. It seemed almost dusty. Like he had walked out of an old Western. Great, she was with John Wayne in the forbidden forest. She chuckled at her thought and then looked up at Annais. Only a couple words had passed between them, but she felt completely at ease.

"I'd be most pleased if you would share with me your reason for coming," Annais said without pretense.

Share with him? Tawly thought, somewhat incredulously. *What might I have to say which Annais had not already heard?*

"You'd be surprised," he retorted, quite playfully.

This was altogether different than Tawly had imagined. She had envisioned stepping into a formal office, going through a pre-screening to see if she was worthy enough to speak to Annais, and then if she passed, having a very intense closed-door session with the powerful leader. Now she felt like she was at an outdoor restaurant that served up food and country music under the stars.

Annais sensed her questions and led with some assuring words:

"You see, Tawly, this is one of my Gathering Places. I tend to favor the outdoors. So my Gathering Place is here. Unless there is danger present. And then I have a slightly more sophisticated arrangement."

"So you live under these trees?" Tawly blurted out.

"No, my dear," Annais replied. "This is one place of many. This is just one where I thought you'd be most comfortable."

At once, Tawly sensed the intelligence of Annais.

Of course you did, she thought.

With Annais seated opposite her at the picnic table, she took her first long look at him. There was nothing formal or arrogant about this guy. There was no staff. He did not have an entourage or Secret Service. The idea of snipers hiding in the trees did occur to her, though. Again, Annais was grinning.

How could this guy rule the Next Place?

Tawly could not stop the question from surfacing and lowered her head immediately, as she knew Annais had perceived her query. But rather than rebuke her, he reached for her hand, gave her a reassuring squeeze, and then tilted his head back and roared with laughter. At some point, Tawly started laughing too. And as she laughed, all the angst she had toward Annais began to fade away. She felt the way you do when you realize the person you are with is turning into a new friend. It was an exquisite feeling, really. And she now wanted nothing more than to sit here and talk late into the night with Annais. But after he quit laughing, he changed moods hurriedly.

"Now that we got that out of the way," he said with a wink, "why don't you get to your question for me?"

Sensing that Annais had somewhere else to be, Tawly decided to be direct and bold about the Destroyer. But before a word came out, Annais stopped her and spoke first:

"My dear Tawly, first, I should tell you that it is apparent from the fierce energy which you bring with you that you spent a good deal of your life and passion taking care of those who were entrusted to you in the First Place. Well done. I have read your story and can only tell you that my heart burst with pride when I finished it."

My story? Tawly thought, balking at this notion.

She had heard it rumored that they all had books which chronicled their life stories somewhere. This seemed far-fetched in itself. But Annais had read them? This she found ludicrous. But when she looked over, and he raised those eyebrows of his and smirked a bit, she knew it was true. He had read her story.

"But that is not all I wanted to tell you, Tawly. I also want to be sure you understand that there is no time that I am not available to you here in the Next Place. Your mission is critical. Your role is irreplaceable. The outcome is imperative. We must win."

Oh, so now came the serious part, thought Tawly. *Great.* She raised her head. Annais was smiling again. *What was it with this guy?*

"Okay," she said, her voice breaking, "then if it is so important that I save Janey, why on earth would you pit me up against that vile, unspeakable Destroyer? I know he tried to destroy me too."

There it was, not prettied up like she had imagined, and not clever like she had planned. But rather desperate and without any eloquence, she had asked the one question she had been filled up with for the last day or so. The one thought which had made the coffee taste lackluster and the falling snow seem less than miraculous. It had followed her around since she had watched that creep leave the night before. And now she had spit it out at the ruler of this Next Place with all the practice of a seven-year-old child. No pretenses.

"None required with me," Annais said simply. "Straightforward is the quickest way to your destination. And here is my answer: It is quite unfortunate that you must face Abaddon again."

His name is Abaddon? Tawly thought as she cringed. *What a horrifying name. Sounds like a dragon. Or a gangster. Fitting,* she supposed.

Annais went on:

"For this, I am sorry. However, in life, you were closer to Janey than anyone else was. You saw her through many of her crucial life junctures, you applauded her life accomplishments, and you sat by as her lifelong relationships took shape. You, quite frankly, are perfectly groomed and suited to be Janey's Keeper. As for Abaddon, well, there is never an easy mission. Only one that is attainable, if you are properly equipped. This, my most precious Tawly, is where your unique ability and your own talents come into play. There is no one else who can do this for me. All my trust is placed in you, alongside the confidence that you will conquer Abaddon. This is a key victory. Don't let me down. I need you, Tawly."

This last statement shook Tawly. It seemed a juxtaposition. How could the ruler of the Next Place need her? But if he did not, why would she be here? Ah, no time for circular reasoning. She glanced up; sure enough, Anais was smiling again.

"I will do my b-b-best," she stammered.

"Quite fair," Annais replied with a chuckle. "How could I ask for more?"

And grasping her across the table, he smothered her in one of those same bear hugs he had greeted her with. And then he was gone. Only the scent of cedar and sage remained. And an afterglow of his presence.

Twyjan

Before Tawly could take another step in Annais's dreamy outdoor Gathering Place, she was back at her own. Staring at the fireplace, she felt the burden of her question gone, but she had a new sensation: one of missing Annais.

Well, that is silly, she told herself.

"No. Not at all," she heard from behind her.

It was Twyjan. Great, from one mind reader to another. A person could not get a thought in around here, without some feedback.

"Well, what does that mean?" she asked with a smile.

She felt relieved to see Twyjan, someone familiar, someone who knew what she was struggling with.

"Everyone comes back from Annais," he said, "wishing they could have stayed with him. But the feeling eventually passes and the reassurance enters in. You will see him again. And that is enough to know for sure."

Well, Twyjan had not steered her wrong thus far. And, because she knew what she knew now, she knew he would not be here if he would. More circular reasoning, it was enough to make her nauseated.

"I need a cup of coffee," Tawly declared. "Pronto."

"Your wish is my command," he said, presenting her with a steaming cup of coffee in her favorite ceramic mug with just the right amount of heavy whipping cream stirred in.

She looked at him quizzically.

"I saw you arrive back," Twyjan said, smiling. "And just knew what you might be needing."

She ambled over to the nearest blue velveteen couch and snuggled in as Twyjan sunk in close by. They had a view of the common room and of the fireplace, and as Tawly looked around, she noticed that everyone seemed in a jovial mood.

"There was just a white fire," Twyjan explained.

"Oh?" Tawly said. "And what exactly does a white fire mean?"

She wasn't sure she wanted to know. She was sort of spent from the last day and all she had learned. She just wanted coffee and quiet. But alas, Twyjan loved the chance to explain things to others, and he seized on the opportunity:

"Well, when someone is saved back on earth, you know, when a Keeper wins the battle against their Loser's Destroyer and they are safe, well, then all the fireplaces in the Next Place turn to white flames. So that everyone can celebrate together."

He seemed so pleased with himself and this bit of information, Tawly noted. She then recognized the true look of celebration on everyone's faces, as if each had a new reserve of hope in their tanks. Something they each needed, no matter what their individual mission. Which brought Tawly's focus back to Twyjan. Realizing she did not know what his current assignment was, she decided to solicit a bit of information about him:

"Tell me, Twyjan: What is it like for you?"

"Do you mean 'What is it like to be a Taker?'" he asked.

"Yes, that. And do you know who you will be taking from earth next?" Tawly added.

"Oh, certainly. In fact, we are given material on our prospect weeks in advance of their departure."

"Material? What kind of material?" she asked.

He paused, looked into her eyes, and said, "I perceive that Annais spoke of your story."

"Yes," she said. "Have you read it?"

"Well, not yours. No, indeed. I have only read those whom I have been assigned to."

"Wow, as in a real book? Like the kind you can hold in your hand?"

Tawly was trying to picture a very voluminous book that held the memory of her life on earth. This was a stretch.

"Yes, it is indeed a book."

"Written?" she insisted.

"Well, yes. Written."

"But how can that be?" she asked. "They are still alive; their story is not finished."

"Ah, this is true. But every moment until then is recorded," Twyjan replied firmly.

"And so, you are granted access to their unfinished story?"

"Yes. I must be. Or I would in no way be prepared to usher them out of the First Place. You see, Tawly, as Takers, we are called to be hyper-vigilant to every emotion that the one departing might be experiencing. And since what they are experiencing could be related to any one experience or occasion in their lifetime, we must be apprised of that in advance."

Well, that seems a little extreme, Tawly thought. Of course, Twyjan read her mind.

"It is a very serious business to be the usher to the Next Place," he replied, rather sternly. "There is only one perfect way to take someone to the Next Place. I must ensure they are escorted along that path."

"Oh. Wow," Tawly said, eying Twyjan. "That sounds wrought with peril."

"Not if you have been prepped," he volleyed back.

"Okay, so you are currently reading someone's story in order to prepare," Tawly reiterated. "But I wonder why they picked you, rather than me."

"Well, I have not heard it spoken of officially, but you will start to notice a trend." Twyjan's voice seemed to drop a decibel.

"Oh? How so?" Tawly asked, sounding less than convinced.

She knew that Annais had his reasons but doubted they could be perceived so easily. Twyjan sensed her doubts:

"You are right, these are only trends. But there must be some truth to them. For instance, I would guess that you are an artist, right?"

"Well, how on earth did you know that?"

"On earth, I would not have," Twyjan joked, unable to resist the easy joke. "But I could surmise that now, because Keepers are called to communicate beauty and hope back to those in the First Place. There is an inherent ability that artists cultivated on earth. It was learned over a lifetime, or perhaps they were born with it. It is not lost, Tawly. Nothing is lost that was created in the First Place. And so, in the Next Place, you might very well find that many Keepers were artists on earth."

Tawly's head was spinning a bit. Too much caffeine, she chided herself. Then she said, "Okay, well, then, what about the Takers: Were you a great group of infamous bandits before your arrival here?"

Twyjan did grin. But he quickly resumed his conspiratorial posture and tone.

"Quite the opposite. I was often the one who was in the shadows. The one who was always watching. Always listening. Detail-oriented to a fault. Crazy compassionate. I was often panged and affected by the smallest of afflictions that another person would suffer. And I was as straight-laced as they come. There was a right and there was a wrong, and I did not cross the line either way."

Tawly watched Twyjan with great intensity.

"Well, at least that is my specific story," Twyjan said. "I was diagnosed with Asperger's syndrome on earth, but I would have described it differently. I was affected by every sound, emotion, and event that happened around me. So much so that sometimes, I could not even speak. But I never missed a beat. I saw and perceived everything, all at once."

Tawly thought back to her Taker. Really, she did not recall any conversation, but Tawly remembered her face so vividly. In her face, she saw what Twyjan had spoken of: an absolute presence and empathy. Her Taker had definitely not missed a beat. If Tawly, then still Iris, blinked an eye, her Taker had noticed. She was the most perceptive and most beautiful thing Iris had ever met. At that time, Iris was not even sure that her Taker was a person. But now that Iris was Tawly, she understood. Her Taker was a person, but a whole person, brought to the Next Place, healed in the Next Place, and given a mission fit just for her that she was fully engaged in. No wonder she seemed so beautiful. Now, the conversation with Annais was coming back to her. Annais had left her with words that seemed to echo Twyjan's theory:

I have planned this out for you to do in advance, but only you can fulfill this undertaking. I need you, Tawly.

All of a sudden, Tawly felt exhausted. She looked up at Twyjan. He was yawning. They exchanged knowing glances and a promise to meet soon.

"Be well, fierce Tawly," he threw over his shoulder.

Tawly stole the chance to watch Twyjan depart. At their first meeting, she had been amused with his tousled hair and wild-eyed look. But now, it was becoming more and more brilliant. She now saw Twyjan as a studied professor of those he would take. His subjects, so to speak, were so much more than that to him. Twyjan was so sincere in his study and his execution that Tawly felt a new respect for him. Indeed, he was odd and quirky, but perhaps, this was just the resin of the genius on the inside, which made him a formidable Taker.

Tawly

Tawly began to snake her way toward the back of the chalet. She peered out the windows as she sauntered by, reviewing the day's events. She knew she was tired, but something Twyjan had said had given her a second wind. Still, she wanted to walk to her bedroom. It was, after all, the type of room she had coveted her whole life. She stepped across the threshold and appreciated it for a moment. The stars shone through the skylights and a band of tall trees stood just outside her wall of windows. The moon was showing off its entirety as it waxed for the last night in its cycle. Tawly had noticed that many of the cyclical patterns were present in the Next Place as well. Waxing moons, day and night, and even the seasons she had sensed were changing. The snow was still coming, but it seemed wetter these days. She had not known whether this would happen or not. There was so much they told you at the beginning. But there was so much they did not. It was a new adventure, even if just to discover that some things were exactly as they had been in the First Place.

Peering out those darkening windows, Tawly began to review her day once more. Such deep and impactful conversations with Annais and Twyjan. Something about Twyjan knowing she had been an artist on earth, even though he knew nothing of her life there, was drumming up new thoughts. She began to make connections between what Twyjan had surmised and what Annais had told her. And then it was clear: what to do next. Tawly stole one last glance of the moon showing off, and then she closed her eyes, inhaled, and slowly exhaled.

When she opened her eyes back up, she was in Janey and Gwin's backyard. Just as Tawly had hoped, the house was dark and empty. The sun was setting behind the back deck, and dusk would slowly dissolve into the deeper night. Tawly figured they had less than an hour before total darkness. She looked into her vision of Janey and saw that her and Gwin were on their way back from a nearby town. Holly. It was just a ten-minute drive from the house.

How serendipitous, she thought.

And then she wondered if there was any such thing. Maybe serendipity had something to do with Annais. Or what Twyjan had spoken of. And then she decided it did not matter. She willed herself into the trees on the side of the road, just a few hundred feet from where her daughter and granddaughter were stopped at a red light. She held her breath as she looked around for what she was counting on. And then something occurred to her: Her breath had carried over to the Next Place. She never felt short of it, however. And considering that was how she had died—and how everyone essentially dies: the actual effect of no breath left - this struck her as a miracle. Of course, it was all miraculous, this whole Next Place. But this little thing struck her now, and she exhaled just because she could. She grinned and then held her breath again as she searched the nearby brush. There they were. Serendipity? Surely not a second time, she surmised. Two of the most splendid deer she had ever seen were gazing right at her.

She didn't quite know how it worked, but she looked at them and said, "Yes, go."

And after their eyes bore back into hers for a second, they turned and leaped in unison toward the road, the road that Janey was driving home on and would be coming to in just seconds.

Tawly's next move was to warn Janey. "Look up, Janey," she said aloud. "Move slowly through the intersection."

Tawly watched as Janey hesitated at the green light. Janey looked at her radio as if she had heard something, paused, and then she began to move like molasses through the intersection. The timing was perfect. In the waning light, the deer looked almost magical. They bounded toward the road and passed about twenty feet in front of the car. The arching jumps, the white tails, and the way they seemingly flew across the road even made Tawly's jaw slack. They were astonishing. And they had affected Janey and Gwin in the exact manner Tawly had hoped. Gwin was jumping up and down in the back seat, and Janey—without doing it on purpose—was grinning from ear to ear. It was one of those smiles that settles your soul, reminds you that all is well, even when it doesn't seem quite so. And now, Tawly exhaled for real. A breath of relief. Her very next thought was of her exquisite bedroom. And she was gone.

Abaddon

Abaddon arrived just two minutes after Tawly had left Janey's house. He deemed this was his most opportune time of day to work. He thought back to the night he started to speak to Jane, the night he found her out walking at her dad's place. He smiled at the memory of her standing still in the street. She had looked like a lost puppy. He figured that lasted a good couple of days: the sting of believing that you were useless. His mouth began to water just a little as he thought about what other worth he could wash away tonight. Jane would not want to see the light of day in the morning. With that thought, he noted that the darkness was creeping in to push away what little light remained. He rolled the metaphor around his dark mind. That was precisely what he was going to do to Jane, he figured. Yet, when Jane pulled in the driveway and got out of the car, he sensed something was amiss.

There's a smile on her face, Abaddon thought. *How could that be?*

Abaddon figured it must be that meddling Tawly. If only he had finished her off when she was younger, none of this would have had to happen. Abaddon watched angrily as Jane and Gwin went into their house and began to settle in. He was thinking up which way he would ruin Jane's good mood when he saw her stop in front of one of her mother's paintings. It was striking, he had to admit. Two deer, in mid-flight, leaping across a country road. Tawly had painted some amazing pieces on earth. Abaddon's first thought was fire. He could set the little house on fire when no one was home. It would be easy enough to make it look like an accident. That way, there would be no trace of Tawly's art remaining. Ah, what a void that would leave. He almost giggled at this thought and started to plan his arson. It wasn't his specialty, though, so he might need to cajole one of the other guys to help him out. Easy enough. Everyone back at camp wanted to be just like him, he assumed. He was sort of doing a pre-celebration as he finalized his plan to burn as much of Tawly's art as he could find. But as if she heard his very plan, Jane made a move which caught Abaddon by complete surprise. After she got Gwin settled in front of the TV, she had taken that deer painting down, taken a picture of it on her camera phone, and walked straight to the computer, where she googled "Tattoo artists who specialize in color and art near Fenton Michigan."

Abaddon cringed at the thought and rolled his eyes. His thoughts got sporadic:

She wants those deer emblazoned on her body. She wants a tribute tattoo.

What gave her this absurd idea? She was going to get a memory of her mom, her art to be precise, and she was going to tattoo it right onto her own body.

Well, that might lift her spirit for a long time. Days, weeks, maybe even years. It would serve as a constant reminder of Tawly's love, beauty, and art, and it would follow her and stay with her no matter what.

Abaddon didn't like this one bit. Jane even had a smirk on her face. This was ruining his whole night. He could no longer think straight. He needed to go back. His eyes became slits as he took one last glance at the leaping deer in the painting, and then he was gone—leaving Jane to the glow of her computer and the list of search results to sift through.

9

Tawly

Tawly woke up feeling a bit of bliss. She had lain in her bed for longer than usual and recounted the night before. It made perfect sense that the animals could help her soothe Janey. Why hadn't she thought of it before? In her life on earth, Tawly had always figured that being surrounded by other living things (other than human) was good for the soul. She just had not thought to ask for their help sooner. But after she had learned how to influence a person's thoughts and after the discussion with Annais about knowing Janey better than anyone, and then when Twyjan mentioned her being an artist … well, the idea of the deer had come to her. And how beautifully it had all played out. Tawly was starting to feel like maybe she could win this war. She hadn't even noticed Abaddon around since the night she saw him on the rooftop, and she certainly wasn't going to wish to run into him.

She grabbed for one of the many goose down pillows, which her bed here was chock full of. Something about the action of a pillow being stuffed underneath her transported her back to the last days she spent on earth. In the hospital bed. Adjusting her pillows: that was what the nurses were always doing. It was as if they knew there was little else that could be done. Iris's temporary comfort in the bed had been their number one priority. At the time, Iris had known what they knew as well. When they had situated her pillows so fastidiously, she had seen their despair mixed with their valiant attempt to get the pillows just right.

There was that time when her whole family was in her room, surrounding the bed, and they were about to put her on the ventilator. Life support. It was protocol for the family to say goodbye, just in case the patient did not come off of life support.

The one nurse had clutched that pillow behind Tawly's head as Tawly had looked at her and said, "If I can't come back off the life support, will I die?" Her eyes had been searching as she was speaking.

But everyone in the room knew it was a rhetorical question. A desperately-seeking-a-different-answer kind of rhetorical question. But rhetorical nonetheless. Everyone had held their breath. But they couldn't hold it forever. They would have to exhale and resign themselves to fate. They couldn't quite look at each other as the doctors and nurses started to create their commotion around the bed, beginning to edge the family out. Iris had seen her answer in the nurse's tear-filled eyes. And she had turned to look at Janey. And Janey had looked back at Iris. For what might have been forever, they had stared at each other.

Tawly could feel the weight of that stare on her chest even now, sitting in her bed in the Next Place. There were moments in your life on earth which would last forever. That was one of them for Tawly. Tawly wondered if Janey ever thought of that moment. The beautiful moment during the horror of the hospital. She hoped she did ... that she maybe even talked about it, maybe with her two lifelong best friends: Elaina and Maggie. The three of them had always been so close. Which made Tawly wonder now:

Had she seen Janey with Maggie or Elaina lately?

She couldn't remember seeing Janey on the phone with them. Maybe she texted them a lot. She resigned to find this out. And then another hospital bed memory surfaced. This one was of Janey's best friend Maggie.

Maggie and Maggie's mom had stopped by one day when Iris was in the hospital. Iris had been embarrassed about not having any hair and about the strange machines in her room. She had always been shy and self-conscious in life, but this brought a whole new level of embarrassment. She was far from the sanctuary of her own home, which she wondered if she would ever see again to top it all off. But she had watched Maggie be a great friend to Janey her entire life and decided she was willing to trust her in this place too. So she lifted her eyes and nodded as Maggie promised over the unrelenting sound of the oxygen machine that she and her mom would take care of Janey if it was Iris's time to go. It was a true relief to Iris at the time, as her options were becoming fewer each day. And Janey was the one she had been worried the most about as she contemplated dying. Janey had always acted like the untouchable one. But she had relied on Iris in a childlike way, even as an adult. And Iris knew, even then, that if she died, it would be a tsunami-size wave in Jane's life. And it would be a flat-out miracle for her to surf over it.

Tawly turned this memory over in her head, sitting in this new bed now, wondering just what to do with this latest thought. And then it hit her: She would take Maggie up on that promise. *I must be able to*, she thought excitedly. She decided she would even skip coffee and head right back to the First Place to find Maggie. Tawly imagined Maggie's face and closed her eyes. When she opened them, she found herself in Brighton at a Michael's store. She spotted Maggie turning the corner into the paint aisle near the back. *I should have guessed*, she quipped to herself.

Art had become Maggie's new haven from the hurt of her father's death. He had died suddenly six months before, when Iris was still undergoing chemo, and all the signs had still pointed to her making a long-lasting recovery. Iris had been shocked, unsettled, and saddened when Maggie's dad died. And it had made her wonder how her own battle would end. Now, as Tawly watched Maggie at Michael's, she ruminated on the idea that Maggie was a lot like Iris. Shy, sweet to a fault, and with a lot of art pent up inside her. She watched Maggie tossing paints into her cart: Everlasting Black, Primordial Purple, and Burnt Sienna. Tawly's mouth watered a bit. This had been one of her favorite haunts on earth: the oil paints section at Michael's. This gave Tawly an idea. Maybe she could speak to Maggie in their common tongue: art. It was a stretch, but Tawly was getting good at making things up as she went now. *Why not?* she thought.

Tawly began to conjure up a vision of two little girls, each walking down the same road from separate directions. They were alone on this old country road. Tawly envisioned the road that split the distance between Janey and Maggie's childhood home: Tipsico Lake Road. It was one reason the girls were fast friends: They were both from the boondocks. It was such a pretty country road, but in this picture Tawly was painting, it was also a formidable road. And the girls were walking more and more slowly with every step. They almost seemed to be receding within themselves. They looked so fearful that they appeared like small wild animals. Until the moment when they accidentally bumped into each other. And then they looked at each other for a time. And the one little girl reached out her hand. And the second little girl took it. This was the best metaphor Tawly could draw in her mind of Janey needing Maggie right now. She just hoped it would work. Tawly held her breath. She was watching from around the corner.

She saw Maggie stop what she was doing and look into the distance, past the paints, past the present.

Maggie had seen it! Tawly knew now that she could also speak to people with pictures, not just words. Maggie must have seen the two little girls appear in her mind's eye and made the connection. And she apparently decided that she must go visit Janey right away. Maggie threw the paints, which she had been debating about as if they were so paramount, carelessly into the plastic basket. She then paid for them and took off in her big, black SUV for Fenton. Forgetting her schedule. Forgetting her grocery list. Forgetting herself, really.

Jane

Maggie was affable, all the time. And all the time, Maggie was affable. It was like a by-law of the friendship between her, Elaina, and myself. But certain circumstances can change these types of certainties. For my Maggie, it was the death of her daddy, which happened suddenly; it was an otherwise normal Monday night and it happened after he dropped his grandson back home after guitar practice. Without forewarning. Without fair notice. And without a farewell. Sure, Maggie had hugged him and thanked him for running her son, Jason, to guitar, but it was a not a thank-you-for-my-life kind of hug.

And she had said: "Good-bye; talk to you later."

But it had not been a good-bye-until-we-meet-again kind of parting. There are game-changers in life. This had been Maggie's. Maggie's dad died six months prior to my own game-changer. When the scene changes in such dramatic fashion in your life, you might just bow out and decide the play is not for you anymore. That had been Maggie. She was not having it. She had been fun, lovable, and affable Maggie all her life. But when her dad died, she was, quite simply, done with the charade. Not only over her father. But over every other misdeed she had suffered in her life, which she had so cleverly hidden under the covers of courtesy and a cheerful demeanor. For once in her life, Maggie had known she had an undeniable reason to be raging mad, and for the first time in her life, she did not care if anyone thought it was justifiable or not. The lid of suppressed emotion had blown right off the top, and she was just begging any one person to call her on it. Except for me, that is. And Elaina. And maybe a couple of other chosen comrades. I had always felt special in Maggie's presence; it was as if she protected me like an older sister. And so, I had tried to help her anyway I could when her daddy had died. I had flown across the country, from Texas where we were living at the time, to try my hand at doing her dishes and sorting her laundry. And I had ended my paltry attempt at comfort by shopping at Target and buying her a photo album for pictures of her dad.

How pathetic, I thought to myself now.

But I could recall my intention. I had felt this deep desire to just sit on the end of her bed until she could wake up without that crushing blow of the morning. Until she could make it outside the shock. But this was not realistic. My husband had been angry at me already. I had needed to keep my job. And my mom had been back in Texas, suffering through her last rounds of chemo. She was headed back to Michigan as soon as her treatment was up, but that was still months away. A part of me wanted to just stay up North and wait. But I could not stay. I knew it, and so, in my place, I would leave a photo album. It had been a stupid idea. I saw it now. What a lousy excuse for a show of sympathy. And I had been kidding myself anyhow. I was completely ignorant when it came to losing a parent. At least, I had been then.

Now, I sat at my mom's old table. In her old kitchen. In her old house. With the smell of the last coffee she had bought running through her old Bunn coffee maker. And this time, it was me waiting on Maggie to come to my rescue. Or at least I thought that's what I was doing. She had called and said something about being in the neighborhood, dropping by, just for a hug. The thought had put pressure on me. Was this how Maggie had felt when I had flown up to see her? I wondered now. Had she felt like she needed to act alive when I got there? I could barely lift my head from staring at the teddy bear salt and pepper shakers sitting on the table in front of me. My mom had bought them when we were together. Somewhere. At thirty-eight years old, I could still take some comfort in teddy bears, at least ones that carried memories of my mom.

When Maggie's Suburban pulled in, I felt a slight shift in my attitude. I took my focus off the table and made my way to the door. Really, there were no words between us. She probably saw me and knew at once what I was feeling. She had a package in her hand. A reusable Target bag with a pink journal and a matching pink pen. And suddenly, some of the shame I felt for my gift given in her grieving was wiped away. I couldn't quite smile, but the top half of my mouth did puff out a little, and my head lifted a few degrees. This was a feeble stand in for my once-upon-a-time, full-face grin. In a show of appreciation for her and her gesture, I walked over to the kitchen counter and pushed Play on my dad's old-fashioned CD player. Maggie had made a CD after her father's funeral with a collection of songs in his memory. She called it *Good Grief*. In the dire weeks leading up to my mom's death, I would listen to a song or two on the way back and forth from the hospital. Most of them were haunting, though, and I had still been in complete denial that my mom was anywhere close to dying. Now, there was only one song I could listen to. Track 12 on Maggie's mixed CD: "Hands," by JJ Heller. I played it now. Gwin twirled in from other room and started in with the chorus:

> *I am trying to understand*
> *How to walk this weary land*
> *Make straight the paths that crooked lie ...*
> *When my heart is breaking*
> *I never leave your hands.*

Gwin had heard it every time we were in the car together for the last few weeks. It seemed like our new anthem. As Maggie's eyes widened into tear-stained pools and I wept, we shared something new: weeping unexpectedly next to each other. I was pretty sure I had never seen Maggie cry. I was absolutely sure I had never cried alongside her. Gwin wanted to hear it again, and so we pressed track 12 again and again. As the lyrics carried my thoughts, I thumbed through my pink journal and wondered if there was one word I cared to write.

Once upon a time, I had savored opportunities to write. At least, before I was relegated to a mute in my grief. It was like a mixed-up version of writer's block. It was ironic that I would question my ability to write in Maggie's presence. She and I had shared the same passion for writing and reading great stuff our whole lives. I recalled us writing each other notes back and forth in middle school. We had both been so shy. It was a time in life when emotions were so raw and unrelenting, and our capabilities to handle them so inadequate. So we would come home from school and unwind by writing notes back and forth in my bedroom. We had met years before in second grade and had flitted through a care free childhood save a brief move on my part to Texas. But even then, we had written. Eight-year-old pen pals. Now, thirty-some years later, we were still pals. And after jaunting around the country for a good part of our adult lives, we had both ended up back in Michigan. There was no longer a need to write letters. I looked at Maggie, and then I looked at my journal: empty. I heard Maggie stand up to grab a tissue and worried that I was a horrible host.

"How are the little ones?" I threw out in desperation.

I was grasping for something that would give me a few minutes to regroup. Maggie just tilted her head and answered me with a half-grin. The one that says "I understand you. I know you. I love you." Before I realized it, she was getting up and heading out.

"Are you headed over to your mom's?" I asked as she gathered her over-the-shoulder purse and surveyed my mother's kitchen for her keys.

"Um, no. My mom is up north at the cabin," she replied, looking at me quizzically.

"Oh? I thought you were in the neighborhood," I said.

Maggie lived thirty miles south in Brighton, but her mom still lived in Maggie's childhood home near Holly, just across town from where my mom and dad had ended up.

"No, not exactly," she said as she shook a confused gaze from her face.

I felt a question linger between us in the early afternoon air. But there was no form to the question, and so I let it go. I watched closely as she backed her big black Suburban out of the driveway, against the backdrop of the budding spring trees and the now melting snow. Once upon a time, that contrast of stark, dark machinery and the soft glory of nature would have held my attention. But now, the poignant scene was wasted on me. I sat down at the table and reflected on how Maggie had always made me feel better. There was no way I was going to write in that journal, though. This much I would have bet my life on.

Tawly

Tawly exhaled audibly as she watched the black Suburban snake out of the neighborhood amongst the trees of her old neighborhood. This was good news. She had been unsure if she could recruit people around Janey. But when the idea had come, she had needed to try right away. As a Keeper, she was not allowed to just remain with her Loser the whole time. That would wear her right out. It would leave the Keepers in the First Place for too long and without the respite they must have. In the Next Place, these things were set in stone by Annais. Tawly wanted to go back and talk to another Keeper about this newfound ability, but she didn't know any by name. She hadn't even caught the name of the one who introduced her to Cato the other day. She had met Raynia, the Mender, and Twyjan, the Taker. And those who had taken and healed her when she had first arrived. But that seemed so long ago, now. And she was not quite sure how to find them. But one thing remained that she knew she could always count on: her Gathering Place. She would go back there now. Perhaps she would get a cup of coffee, sit by the fire, and wait for the right person to show up.

Sorta shady plan, Tawly thought.

But it seemed like the next right thing to do. Tawly decided to take one last look into the window of her old home. She saw Jane and Gwin watching a cartoon on the couch. They seemed safe in their post-Maggie haze, for now. As Tawly gazed in at her daughter and granddaughter, she again reveled in the phenomenon of having her memories of her life as Iris. Because of her memories, she had been able to come up with this idea of recruiting Maggie. Of course, it was Maggie who made the promise, so the idea was Maggie's as well. Although at the time, Maggie probably had no idea what she was signing up for. Tawly laughed at this latest roundabout bout of reasoning. She was half-giddy. It felt so good to be helping her daughter. She wanted to give Maggie a great big hug. It was one of those impulses that stuck from the First Place. The need and the desire to wrap your arms around another. To get your heart as close as you could to their own. But the physical border between the First Place and the Next was impenetrable, as far as Tawly understood.

Oh well, she said to herself. *There is so much to wait and see about.*

And so now, Tawly lowered her eyes and dreamt of the hot steaming java waiting for her under the canopy of majestic pine trees. Only a blink away.

Abaddon

Abaddon wanted a quick fix. Just something to avert his attention from the angelic likes of Tawly and her antics of late. He had been at Tawly's old house, just to mess with Jane a bit. Jane had been at her mom and dad's, which was not really her mom's house anymore. He loved that part and wanted to pour a little salt into the wound of Janey being all alone now that her mother was dead. But out of the blue, that girl Abaddon had never seen had driven up in her big black car, and he'd had to abandon the whole thing. He angered easily, and this had made him madder than he could explain. He'd gone straight back to the one place he could call home: the Camp.

The Camp was in the middle of the forest, and it was just that: a camp. He didn't know how many lived there. It was a huge sea of big black tents. And they all butted up to a clearing, which had a campfire and some picnic tables. Abaddon headed straight for his tent, as he was not exactly in the mood to be social. He was steaming mad. He had calculated that it would only take three visits or so to for him to finish Jane off. He had started in on her the night he found her out walking in the road at her dad's. And he had thought he was on easy street. But Tawly had pulled some trick with the deer painting and the tattoo inspiration and now she had snuck up on him with one of Janey's little friends. It was her nonsensical hope. Abaddon hated the notion of hope the most. He knew it was a bunch of drivel. Hope couldn't drive out the darkness. He knew this because he had been stung by hapless hope when he was young and naïve.

When Abaddon was five, "they" had told him to hold out hope when his mom was dying of a disease that was, in fact, entirely hopeless. But he didn't know that. And so, he had held out for hope. And then, she had died. And he had seen it on their faces as they apologized to him and said how sorry they were that she had not made it. They had lied. And the young Abaddon had seen right through it. He had been given two choices: to believe they lied for his good, or to believe they lied for their own good, for their own comfort. That they had lied because they hadn't wanted to make themselves uncomfortable telling the truth. The latter was the one he felt most comfortable with. The former he found contradictory. How could he have believed someone lying to him was for his own good? His mom's life had ended. He had been deserted, and the truth had been obverted. From then on, he made his choice: To move forward with his own truth. Abaddon vowed that whatever he decided the truth was, it would always be good for him. He would never care about anyone else. After all, this is what they had taught him: Put your own interests first. He hadn't been able to argue with a good old-fashioned example at a mere five years old.

From then on, instead of hope, Abaddon worked strictly with action. He always took matters into his own hands. He didn't need another person to make him feel better or optimistic. In fact, his philosophy was to see the future as he wanted it, to manipulate the pawns around him to get it, and then to dismiss them one by one to their puny little lives while he sat in the king's corner, considering that which he would conquer next. This is what Abaddon's life on earth had turned into at a very young age: a game. Winning was everything. He was addicted to his own audacity. He fed on it. And that same attitude had followed him here.

On the way back to his tent, Abaddon noticed Ike hanging out by the fire. And an idea came to him. Abaddon sauntered up next to Ike. Ike was not the most astute of the Destroyers. Abaddon favored him for this reason. Ike could be persuaded with one word: "money." What Abaddon knew and Ike had yet to figure out was that the currency in the Legion was not money. Certainly, it could get one some fresh tobacco or a bottle of moonshine, but it would never get you closer to the top. And that was the only point in being in the Legion, at least in Abaddon's estimation. He would gladly trade money for power. In fact, it was a real rush to give money to someone like Ike and watch him become a puppet in the master's hands. Abaddon's own, of course.

Ike listened to Abaddon's plan:

"...Let us ambush a strong, young male who is being taken ... serve up a quick defeat to the other side ... have a little fun."

Ike heard these words, but the main thought in his stream of consciousness was a stream of thick liquor running down the back of his throat. He loved the burn of good, hard liquor, and since it cost a pretty penny around here, Abaddon's wish would be Ike's command. As Ike headed out to snatch someone from the Road of the Taken, Abaddon strolled leisurely behind him. Ike seemed to stomp down the road like a Clydesdale horse. The ground broke slightly under each heavy foot, and he swayed from side to side in his lumbering gait. Yet there was a bit of a rocking rhythm to it that made it less than clumsy.

On earth, Abaddon had been told, Ike had been a hockey player. A really good one, at that. Actually, he got so good that at the height of his career, he could have chosen any team in any country to play on. And the team he chose paid him handsomely to call theirs his home ice. But with each new home, the ice that had once brought him passion, energy, and more money seemed like a cold dead end. The shimmering ice, which had once spurred him on, had turned into a melting pool of monotony.

To bust up the boredom, Ike had started to look for thrills in bottles of that which would not freeze over. Slowly, his talent was super-saturated in Russian vodka, Canadian beer, and the finest of

French wines. And then one Sunday at high noon, in a completely drunken stupor, Ike was called on to profit his soul. For all that he had profited thus far, there was nothing he could do. He had drunk himself right to death. And then he had been taken, like every other soul who died before him, down the very trail he and Abaddon were headed to now.

Abaddon sneered at the memory. Ike's unsuspecting Taker had made one false move, and Abaddon had seized the burly Nordic athlete. Fists, words, and even Ike's blood had passed between the Taker and Abaddon, but Abaddon had won. And he had drug Ike off the path and into the deep woods. The ruckus had made Ike think he was back on the ice and was being hauled off to the penalty box for fighting on the rink; perhaps the last bottle of rum had just given him a wicked-bad dream rather than sent him packing for good. But Abaddon was quick to slap that silly thought right off Ike's face.

He had spun him around and said to the stunned new soldier, "Now you belong to the Legion. You will listen to me until you are summoned by the leader and given your first job. Understood?"

Ike had blurted out a bunch of questions: about the leader, about being dead, and about the forest. But he never got any good answers, and Abaddon had laughed at the dumbfounded look on Ike's face. He savored moments like those. Looking at the back of Ike's head now, he surmised that but for the chance at some moonshine, Ike would run away if he could. There were certain trappings which eventually enslaved soldiers of the Legion. Moonshine, the latest weapons, the most exotic foods and spices. And then for those above the fray of these lures, there was always the pull of power. And the Legion spoon-fed that out. If someone was suspected of defecting, the Legion would dole out a promotion. Each step up this ladder was really a descent into a deeper darkness, but this apparent contradiction was just one more way that the Legion tricked its own army. It was just where the Legion wanted them: in the cog of the machine. The upside for the Legion was that the further a soldier fell, the less they thought for themselves. This was exactly what the Legion's leader desired. This way, they would not even consider trying to escape. Abaddon figured if Ike was dumb enough to run, there was really no place to run to anyhow.

There was, however, one underground rumor about escape: The rumor was that one could simply utter the name Annais, and Annais himself would materialize on the spot. But what happened then? Well, the rumors varied wildly from there. No one knew for sure. Annais and everything beyond the forest was a bit of a fairy tale to those in the Legion. They couldn't quite grasp it all. Abaddon thought it was all absolute nonsense. It was unthinkable to him that Annais might come to save one of them. Only an idiot would consider such drivel, he figured.

David

David went temporarily mute when Abaddon and Ike seized him. The suddenness of it all stole his voice and his breath. As Ike walked behind him, prodding him on, and Abaddon walked in front of him, spewing threats along the dimly lit path, David began to recollect how he had ended up in the forest. It felt so distant and radically different from the place he had been walking before, the path he had strayed from with his new friend. Yes, his new friend, Twitter? Timber? Tipper? What was his name? David's thoughts were a mess. That guy had given him such a sense of peace. But this guy, Ali Baba? Ugh, David was bad with names. Didn't matter, this guy scared him to death. Why had he followed him? It was kind of a blur.

He and … Twyjan … yes, that was it, Twyjan had been leading the way down the Road of the Taken (he had told him it was called that), talking to David about his family and all those he had left behind. He had been assuring David that those left behind remained for particular appointments. That it was not all one big disaster. That certain Keepers would be assigned to each of them. The knowledge of this had been an awakening of sorts, after being ripped away from his loved ones in the First Place. It was baffling, but David had begun to settle down. He might even get to meet those who were keeping his loved ones back home, Twyjan had told him.

"What about my big brother?" David had asked Twyjan. "Who will take care of Andy?"

David was fourteen; a car accident had put him into the coma which eventually claimed his life that very morning. But his big brother Andy was sixteen. Andy was at a crossroads at home. He was constantly arguing with their parents and seemed to be in perpetual trouble. David had become Andy's one confidante in the last six months. David felt like a hero when Andy would come to his room seeking solace. And now, David had thought, he would be just one more reason for Andy to sink further into the cave of his depression. This thought had brought tears to his eyes. David had begun slowing down as he thought of him, back home, bewildered by his little brother dying. He had noticed he was losing sight of Twyjan and had started to pick up the pace a little.

"Your leaving will be the last straw. The final nail in his coffin," said a strange voice that had snuck in from the woods.

David had stopped dead in his tracks. Surely Twyjan had not said that, he thought. Then he had checked. No, Twyjan was still walking and had been talking a few meters ahead. David had still been able to hear him faintly ... something about how David would feel very well physically and something about a Gathering Place. They had been so very close to the Gates of the Next Place that Twyjan apparently did not even notice David had faltered. It had been a fatal mistake. The other voice had come back. It was oozing out of the tree line to the right. Could it be telling him the truth? David wondered.

"Your brother will surely die, all because of you," Abaddon had slithered through the space between them. "But if you choose to come with me, I can show you a way to protect him. Twyjan is useless. He's too naïve to know what I know. Only I can show you how to ease your brother's sorrow. And the rest of your family for that matter. Think of your big brother. Just come with me."

David had turned toward the voice. It was the thought of Andy.

If this man could help his brother ... he would do anything, he had thought. Abaddon was in the zone. This was his game, he told himself. He had looked at Ike to make sure he was ready to grab David. Ike had looked a little worried. Abaddon had elbowed him and flashed him a do-or-die look. Ike's shoulders went back, and he got in a ready-to-pounce stance. Abaddon loved Ike's prowess in these situations. Right now, he thought all of the sprinting drills that hockey players had to do were genius. They had unknowingly created a beast for Abaddon to use to his advantage.

He turned back to David just on the other side of the tree line and said, "A few more steps, David, and I will explain it all to you. Yes, I can help Andy feel better. We can fix it all. Yes, there. One more step. You can do it. The choice is all yours: help Andy or leave him to suffer. It is all within you if you just take that one last step."

And then David had. And the regret had been instantaneous. He had turned around, but the path back had disappeared. David had thought he could faintly hear someone screaming his name. But it had been overshadowed by the face of Abaddon, which was now spitting distance from his own. The energy in David's body seemed to have been sucked right from his very core. Abaddon had broken into a sly grin.

"Ah, fear not," he had said. "I will teach you. I have watched you in the First Place. You, too, will be great like me." Abaddon assumed this would be a comforting thing to hear.

"But ..." was the only word David could muster.

David's breath and his energy had all seemed trapped in the box of his body. He could shuffle down the path, but on the inside, he had felt like he was lassoed inside his torso. A beating heart inside a body on autopilot. He had known right then that he had to follow. Like a soldier follows a misguided sergeant into a battle that bodes defeat. No choice. No voice. No chance.

Ike was the one who had taken David's arms behind his back. But Ike had known it wasn't necessary. Ike had fought like his life depended on it when he had been taken. Maybe because he had been trained to fight on the ice. But not this kid. He was scared stiff. And he was too little. As messed up as Ike had become here, he still knew one thing: Abaddon was sick. David was just a kid. Ike had loosened his grip a bit. Abaddon had looked back and told Ike to hurry up if he wanted his money. That was enough to get Ike back in line. He nudged David along, but the bad feeling in his stomach had remained.

The whiskey will help that, Ike heard in his head.

He had figured the voice was right.

10

Tawly

Tawly woke up to a bright and sunny day and with a fresh outlook. She had rolled out of bed and headed straight out to the common room. Looking up at the rafters as the light shone into the hallway that served as the coffee and tea stop, she positively beamed. She recounted in her mind what had happened the day before. Tawly had figured out a way to get Janey's best friend Maggie to go visit her daughter; she thought Janey had seemed calmer and even a bit happier after the visit. This would be a huge asset for Tawly. She could not be by Janey's side all the time. And honestly, most times, she felt a deep need to return to her Gathering Place quite quickly after being back in the First Place. So now she knew she could recruit Janey's friends. At least her two best ones: Maggie and Elaina also, she assumed. And she could probably use the rest of the family too.

Yes, it was all falling into place. She was feeling quite pleased with herself. Tawly was sure that Janey seemed a bit better the last few days; she felt like she was walking on cloud 9. She recalled the recent victories: the orchestrated visit from Maggie, the potential future job for Janey, the interlude with those beautiful deer. Tawly was beginning to think that she could not be stopped now. In her elation and with a piping hot cup of coffee in her hand, she skipped around the corner, out of the coffee galley and into the great room. And there she was stopped. In her tracks, to be precise.

There was a heap of clothing on the floor by the fireplace. *How had I not seen this walking in from the bedroom?* she wondered. There was an eerie noise emanating from the heap. It sounded like a wounded animal. Something was wailing. Drawing closer, Tawly realized that it was not an animal. It was Twyjan. He was curled up in a ball just in front of the fire, which had turned into an eerie bluish color. Tawly ran to Twyjan now, instinctively looking for an injury or some blood. And then she remembered that people did not bleed within the Gates of the Next Place. She was on the floor in no time, next to him, with her hand warming his shoulder. She started to tell him it would be okay, but Twyjan's wailing drowned her words right out:

"David. No. David. Come back. Not that way. I can't see you. You can never come back if you don't turn around … No. David. Not you. I … we …"

Like the chorus to a haunting song, Twyjan started again:

"David. No. David. Come back. Not that way. I can't see you. You can never come back if you don't turn around," the refrain continued.

Tawly felt helpless; a horrific, sinking feeling was spreading from her chest into her throat. And then she heard the door from the outside deck slide open. Annais did not make eye contact with Tawly but was at Twyjan's side in what seemed like two strides. He towered over the man Tawly had come to think of as a confidante and friend. Annais's ox-like strength made Twyjan seem all the more feeble. Annais held him in his arms, like a fallen soldier, and he made for the doorway in a jog. Tawly noticed that Twyjan was clasping a dark blue book to his chest, and his miserable chorus continued. As Annais crossed the deck to descend the stairs into the forest, he looked briefly over his shoulder at Tawly. His eyes seemed almost black; she had thought they were blue the last time they had met. There was not a word between them. But she heard him loud and clear. Annais had told her that Twyjan would need her. And she felt an overwhelming impulse to go to Raynia. What for, she had no clue.

Raynia

Tawly wished right away that Annais had taken her too. How was she supposed to help Twyjan if she did not know where he was? She had wanted to follow Annais, to see how to get to his place from hers. But that was probably a real shot in the dark. She had been told that Annais travelled differently than her. And that was not what Annais had "told" her to do. Sometimes, she wished that she didn't have to read people's minds. She was not all that great at trusting this, just yet.

So what are my other options? she thought in desperation. She looked into the gorgeous great room and, for the first time, found it lacking. It felt tainted. She noticed the coffee she had dropped on the floor when she had spotted Twyjan in the heap of clothes. Such a stark stain against such beauty. Like Twyjan's brokenness amidst the Gathering Place, she thought. She hemmed and hawed and then decided she could at least patch up the visual blemish, collecting her thoughts as she cleaned.

During her life on earth, Tawly had found cleaning to be a cheap form of therapy. Because of her father's alcoholism, he had often lost jobs. And yet, because of his many skills and winning personality, he had always found a new job. Some new jobs were in other towns, though. So her family had always been on the move. And as the oldest child, Tawly had needed to help her mom get the new places in order. Cleaning up and fixing up had become a way of life for her. Like so many other pieces of her personality, Tawly had carried this idiosyncrasy to the Next Place. So as she swept the pieces of the ceramic cup off the knotty pine floor, she began to calm down. She felt her anxiety subside and her breath return (had she been holding her breath this whole time?). And then, a rush of peace saturated her, right to the bone, it seemed. She pivoted on the end of her broom and was face-to-face with Raynia, who was inches from Tawly's face. Tawly had not noticed before, but now she couldn't help noticing: Raynia was emanating an intoxicating fragrance, something made up of sandalwood, earth, and the outdoors in general. Raynia must have just come in from her herb garden. She spent most of her time out there. She often sang as she gardened, and the melodies flitted in on the breeze. The others were soothed whenever her singing reached their ears. Tawly had heard a little about Raynia through the grapevine.

They told her that Raynia had been a nurse in the First Place, but that her true passion had been her garden. By her own admonition, she had been a bit of a tree hugger and was known for her green thumb. In her spare time, she had sought out every book, magazine, and website she could find on what grew best where, when, in which climate, under which sunlight, in which conditions, alongside this or that, how it was best nurtured, and lastly, what it might be useful for. She had started with wild roses and peonies and had branched into chamomile and lavender. And from there, she learned how to use the dried flowers, dried herbs, and the oils that could be extracted from each. She had longed to open an apothecary and had dabbled in mixing her own tinctures. She had tested her potions on her children and on her friends. And then she had sold them at the local market. No one had taken her very seriously, though. Raynia had known something back on earth, where she was called Kathy. She had known that the key to the healing of all things had been provided for in nature. Yet like her least-favorite doctor at the hospital where she had worked, the ego of humankind seemed to deafen any alternative way of thinking. There was this strange notion, oddly accepted by almost everyone, that something manufactured, invented, or made from human hands must be better than nature itself. Kathy had not been sold on this. But she had not been allowed to say so. She had been told to help people, to encourage them to take the drugs the doctors prescribed, and to stay away from her so-called holistic healing ideas. So although her heart was led back to the garden the minute she got home from work, when she went back to work, she had to leave the garden behind. After Tawly heard all of this about Raynia, it was quite obvious why she had been chosen as a Mender in the Next Place and not Tawly. One question answered.

After Raynia walked into the great room, she noticed the blue fire and Tawly's malaise simultaneously. And she had gone straight to her. Tawly blurted out the whole scene in one breath, concluding with Annais carrying Twyjan off.

"What do you make of it?" she asked anxiously.

"Ah. Well …" Raynia seemed hesitant and paused.

She peered over at the fire, which seemed to be turning back to the normal orange flames.

"The blue flames of the fire are a signal that there is danger," Raynia finished.

"What do you mean? I thought we were safe here." Tawly sounded like a child who had been tricked again.

"No, not in present danger," Raynia assured her. "It is not like that. Indeed, we are safe, but there is something greater at stake. And in the ongoing war against the Legion, something has been lost …" Raynia's voice trailed off.

Tawly felt her breath leave again.

"Did they hurt Twyjan?" Tawly spat out.

"No, certainly not," Raynia corrected. "Again, you and I are safe. As is Twyjan. But there are always the others. The ones on earth and the ones in between. The Legion can only affect those people. They place all their efforts there. They believe that the fewer who make it to the Next Place, the better chance they will have in the end."

"The end? What are you talking about?" Tawly demanded.

"That's something which is better explained by Annais. All in time, but for now, I can tell you that Twyjan was somehow involved in a battle. And based on a conversation I had with him, Annais had warned him that the boy he was taking was to be watched very closely."

Raynia was speaking each word as if every syllable was important.

"You mean he was taking a young boy?"

Tawly thought back to her conversation with Twyjan. He had not told her who he was taking.

Raynia knew Tawly was confused and scared. She grabbed her hand and looked her in the eyes.

"Yes, Twyjan had been reading this boy's story for the last month or so. He seemed super enveloped in the book, if you had seen him out and about. Mostly, he has been in his room. He was over studying, in my opinion. He had called on me for some flower remedies to ease the strain on his eyes. He must have read this boy's story three times, just to ensure he did not miss a thing. I do not know what might have gone wrong. But I could guess."

With this, Raynia looked out the window.

Tawly followed her gaze and noticed that the windows in the great room had taken on a depressing gray tint. Tawly's first instinct was that there was a storm coming in, although she had never seen a storm in the Next Place. Raynia's eyes widened.

"Take refuge," Raynia said. "There will be a storm."

She embraced Tawly and then ran out the door. Apparently to cover the newly planted seeds, Tawly figured.

"It will not be pretty," Raynia shot over her shoulder.

What exactly did that mean? Tawly stood there for a second and then figured the great room was as good a place as any to sit out a storm. She had loved the thunder and lightning storms on earth and decided it might be meditative to sit down on the couch, lay her head back, and soak in the sounds of the rain. She quickly scrapped this idea, however, and found herself cowering under the oversized coffee table. When the fast and furious storm finally began to subside, Tawly crawled halfway out from under the long, dark wooden table. How mistaken she had been. Sure enough, the common room had been a safe haven. But it was a far cry from meditative. In all her life in the First Place, she had not witnessed anything like it. It was less intense than a tornado but seemed angrier somehow, as if the elements were taking a beating out on the ground.

She crept all the way out now and moved cautiously to the window on the garden side. As she suspected, Raynia had placed a protective covering over her fragile herb garden before the storm hit. And although the flowers appeared soggy, they had not been torn from their stems. *Odd*, she thought. If a rip-roaring storm of that magnitude had come through on earth, the trees would have been leafless and flowers reduced to mere dust floating in the aftermath. But perhaps the strangest thing of all was that she sensed some sort of relief in the air. Was that just her own angst subsiding?

She looked out at the trees and noticed a deer and its fawn. This was the first time she had spotted deer in the Next Place. She briefly thought of the two she had somehow influenced on earth. How they had seemed to understand her and had jumped across the road, to Janey and Gwin's delight. This made her smile, and she contemplated the wonder of animals. One thing she knew: She was sure glad they were here in the Next Place. The large orbs of the mother deer's eyes sort of transfixed Tawly. She started to wonder about Twyjan again and debated whether she should look for him.

But a voice stopped her: "The Retribution has begun," Tawly heard.

Tawly looked around, but other than the deer, no one was there. And when she looked up, the mother deer had turned and was leaping through the trees, with her fawn behind her. They seemed to be playing, joyfully almost. *I better get some rest*, she thought. *I'm hearing voices now.*

11

Tawly

Tawly strolled along the windowed hallway on her way back to her room. The sky after the storm was a light gray. She had always loved how the air felt and smelled after a storm back on earth. She could smell it here, as well. The outdoorsy smell was cascading in through the open windows. With the snowy mix and the mild temperature, it was sublime. And Tawly couldn't resist: She stepped out onto the deck for a couple breaths of fresh air before she retired to her room. The white tails of the mom and baby deer were still visible, amongst the trees. They were grazing in the distance now. Tawly surveyed the landscape and had decided to go back inside when she heard a very small voice behind her:

"They said, 'The Retribution has begun.'"

"Eh? Excuse me?" Tawly said, not knowing who was talking.

Something rustled behind her. Tawly turned slowly and saw someone in the shadowy corner of the deck. It must be a girl, she presumed from the sweet, light voice. She could make out that she was petite. But she had not moved out of the shadows fully; she seemed wary, so Tawly approached slowly.

The little girl took one step forward. As she came out of the shadows, an iridescent icy blue aura came with her. "I am Zaduk," she said with a mischievous smile.

Tawly wondered what this girl was out here doing. Maybe she had been sent by someone to check on her? Had Raynia sent her? *Or perhaps she had just been trying to frighten me to death,* Tawly thought.

"Well, hello," Tawly said, smiling instinctively and thinking how cute this girl was.

Zaduk was wearing a red cape, woven with many beads and metals, and even some leaf-like material. She had the most spectacular hiking boots, and snowshoes were fastened to her backpack. Her cheeks were bright red, and she had a wildness about her that was positively exuberant. But Tawly wondered what this Zaduk was talking about. Her brain was spinning, and she was not in the mood to do any sort of guessing. So she walked over, shook Zaduk's hand, and then just looked at her. It had been quite a morning; Tawly was hoping Zaduk had something comforting to say.

"I just wanted to let you know what the deer said to you," Zaduk said in a matter-of-fact tone.

"Oh, well, I guess I was questioning my sanity, anyhow. Did the deer really speak?" Tawly asked.

"Yes, of course," said Zaduk. "You just were not paying attention to them, which is common when you first arrive here. With time, you will become more adept at interpreting what they are saying to you."

"Okay, so … you have been here a while?" Tawly queried.

"Ah, well, not as long as many of the others," she replied, "but I had a bit of a head start in the First Place."

"A head start? Doing what?" Tawly ventured.

"Understanding the animals," Zaduk answered. "I just mean, in the First Place, I was raised in South Dakota, on my family's farm."

"Can't take the country out of the girl," Tawly said, chuckling, "even when you leave the earth."

Zaduk grinned at Tawly's silly joke. Tawly noticed her ice blue eyes atop that big grin. Zaduk had some bright blonde hair peeking out from under her woolen hat; Tawly wondered how a Scandinavian girl from the plains ended up with a Gathering Place that was more like a mountain hideout than a farm.

As per usual, Zaduk read Tawly's mind and then answered with a pained expression:

"I experienced great sorrow on the farm. My little sister died in a combine accident," she said. "And so, when I was old enough, I took a trip to Colorado, and, well, I fell in love with the mountains and all the snow. It was different enough to help me forget. And yet, I always felt closer to her there."

Tawly was starting to get it.

"So are you a Keeper of animals?" Tawly ventured.

"Ah, no," Zaduk said. "I guess you have not heard of my kind. I am a Teller. We are trusted with communicating with the animals here. We are translators between them and those who do not understand them."

"So the animals told you about whatever just happened with the storm?" Tawly asked, sounding skeptical.

Tawly knew she had been able to influence the deer back home, but that they might have some sort of language seemed a little hokey.

"Oh certainly," she said. "They understand Annais in a most intimate way. They sense things he does before we do. Sometimes, in fact, like you just witnessed, it is they who tell us what is going on. And then we Tellers relay the message. The deer, in particular, are incredibly perceptive. I always look to them first when there is a storm of any kind."

"Well, then I guess I wonder just one thing," Tawly said, looking at Zaduk.

"Sure, shoot," she said in a very no-nonsense tone.

"Retribution for what and to whom?" Tawly was not sure she wanted a response, but it was out there now.

Zaduk contemplated her words before she spoke:

"Well, I do not know the full story. No one does. But what I do know is that the Legion stole someone who was headed here. Annais is incredibly busy, unless something happens to one on the way. And then he cannot be ignored. No one can escape when Annais has been wronged. And nothing provokes him more than when the Legion steals someone who is on their way here."

Tawly was like a little child who didn't quite get the way things work: chock full of questions and short on patience for answers. She started in again:

"Well, what does his revenge look like?"

Tawly could not imagine that the grandfather-like figure she had encountered could be vengeful.

"This is not ours to understand," Zaduk said, "nor to be informed about. What I do know is that his first priority is the one whom the Legion took. After that, it is anyone's guess what Annais might do to equalize the evil deed of the Legion."

"So he will be able to save this person?"

Tawly was starting to feel a little better and wanted some certainty. But she was disappointed when Zaduk said, sounding exasperated, "Again, anyone's guess."

Zaduk heard a call out in the woods. Tawly would have sworn it was a coyote, which made her want to run inside. But it had the opposite effect on Zaduk, who said she would go and then headed to the edge of the deck. They promised to meet for coffee soon, and Tawly watched her skip off the deck into what was turning into a bright sky. As she disappeared between the trees, Tawly watched the beauty of nature envelop her and wondered aloud if the animals on earth might be able to tell things too. Or if instead they might be able to understand her words. She didn't know. But it was one more thing she wanted to find out. She deliberated for a moment. Her curiosity would not quit, though. So she closed her eyes and decided to go back to the First Place to check for herself. She ended up just outside Janey's house, but in the backyard this time.

Tawly glanced in through the back patio door and saw her daughter eating with little Gwin. As was her habit of late, Janey was not actually eating, but rather just sitting at the table, as if she was fooling anyone. Even Gwin, who was so young, would look at her mom occasionally and wonder why she only stared blankly at her plate. Gwin had been forced to learn how to start a conversation when the chatter was otherwise dead-on-arrival between them. At a mere three years old, she was learning to be the social instigator in her relationship with her very own mom. Tawly sighed and wondered if her earlier optimism was premature. Maybe every time she went back to the Gathering Place feeling giddy, Janey slumped back into this abyss of barely-there. Tawly spotted a bright red cardinal with one of those brilliantly yellow beaks on the snowy deck and remembered why she had come here. This was just what she needed. He was hopping to and fro, apparently looking for food, and as she got closer to him, she tried to be keen to any sound he was making. He started to sing, as she remembered the birds on earth singing. Sure enough, she could not hear the bird "speak" to her in anyway, as her new friend Zaduk had described. Tawly apparently needed some practice with this.

If only I could ask him to sing outside the kitchen window, she thought.

Tawly longed in her heart to see Janey smile. She watched Janey get up from the dining room table and approach the deck's sliding door. Suddenly, the stunning cardinal flew onto the chair nearest the door. Janey opened the door and took a deep breath. She then gasped at the proximity of the cardinal. He had perched just two feet away, smack dab on that chair, and burst into song. Tawly swore the volume had tripled from his earlier singing. Janey quickly and quietly urged Gwin over to the half-open deck door. Fearing he might dart for the nearest tree, Tawly held her hands together over her heart as the most unlikely thing happened: Gwin ran outside and put her face quite close to the bird. And the cardinal remained in that very spot. One might have thought there was a program of music that the bird had agreed to perform, as he finished with the same gusto. With a final splendid note, he leaned forward into little Gwin's face and then took off into the bright winter sky. Gwin stood there, gaping, with her head cocked back and watched the cardinal career out of sight. When he had disappeared, it started to feel a bit chilly for being out on the deck in pajamas, so Janey grasped Gwin's little hand and turned around to return to the kitchen table. Tawly took one last look at the back deck door and now felt entirely spent. She was about to close her eyes and go back to the lodge when she heard the snow crunch behind her. She swiveled around to see a flutter of red over the fence. Must have been a squirrel, she guessed. And she left without another thought.

Jane

I was still shaking my head as Gwin sat back down to her bunny pastas and carrots. I had never seen a cardinal that close, nor had I ever felt like one had serenaded me. That was exactly what had just happened to Gwin, who seemed to be happy but not overly blown away by the whole incident. It was as if, in her world, it were quite common to commune so closely with the birds. I thought it was awfully strange, though. It felt orchestrated. Yet Gwin had started eating again and seemed oblivious. I smiled at her innocence. As I was sitting down, something else caught my eye in the backyard. If I was honest with myself, I thought it was a small girl; she wore a wool cape and snowshoes, and was escaping out our back gate. I shook my head and closed my eyes, thinking I might fix my own vision. When I opened them, there was nothing there. *Good grief,* I scolded myself, *I need my head examined.* Certainly no one was out snowshoeing in our backyard. And then I convinced myself that this, too, I had made up, that I was just longing for my mom. Maybe I was regressing into my weird visions. Or maybe someone from Child Protective Services was watching me. Who knew? I would not have blamed them. I was certifiable, by my own admission. I looked up again. Whoever or whatever it was, they were gone now. And Gwin needed to finish her lunch. So that I could get her down for a nap. So that I could get to my one respite: my bed, my mom's shawl, and the nether land of sleep.

12

Twyjan

Twyjan awoke on his back. He instinctively clutched his chest, but the book was gone. He sat straight up and looked around in a panic. There was a table next to the long leather bench he had been lying on. And there was the book. David's name was etched along the binding, and the silver letters gleamed in the room's low light. Twyjan's eyes moved around the room as he tried to piece together what had happened. Last he remembered, he had heard Tawly's voice and then felt the unmistakable presence of Annais. Now, he found himself alone in this unfamiliar room. There was a candle chandelier above him and a fireplace. But no other lights. Twyjan surmised it was night. One night, to be precise, since he had lost David. This thought made him hang his head and made his chest feel like it would collapse right into his back.

"It is not over; do not lose heart, Twyjan." Annais spoke from somewhere behind him.

Twyjan lifted his head and felt his lungs fill back up with air. He turned slightly and saw Annais striding over to him. Annais sat down on the coffee table. Twyjan had always loved how casual he could be. He felt so at ease with him. Annais bent over with his elbows on his knees, clasped his large hands together, and looked directly at Twyjan. Even in this low light, Annais's eyes had a reflective quality. They were green, at least today. Twyjan had seen Annais once when his eyes appeared almost black; he shook the thought of that night off. For now, Annais seemed absolutely harmless. And Twyjan somehow felt everything was going to be okay. With no clue how it would be okay, but it would, this he just felt.

"I am so sorry, Twyjan," Annais said with intense sincerity.

"No," Twyjan began, hanging his head again. "It is I who should be sorry. I just thought we were there and … well, I was so happy I had gotten him home, and he was feeling so much better … and then I got overly excited and was just talking and …" Twyjan's voice trailed off.

He looked up. He looked past Annais this time to the fireplace and got lost in the flames, recalling the back of David's head as he slipped off the path.

"Twyjan, I know this will be most difficult. But I have to ask you some pointed questions about David."

Twyjan looked scared. And Annais knew it. He said reassuringly, "I am not angry with you, Twyjan. There is nothing I will scold you about, nor do I wish to make you feel worse than you already do. But there are some things I must know."

Twyjan's shoulders dropped; he looked earnestly at Annais and said quietly, "Yes, anything."

"I must know what you told David to this point."

"Well, I don't know; what do you mean? I told him the normal things: that he was to be healed, that it was not all one big disaster. That him leaving would not make his brother give up …" Twyjan was just getting rolling.

But Annais stopped him:

"Ah ha. And so, he was worried about those back in the First Place."

"Well, yes, of course. He was worried about his big brother, Andy. He felt that his car accident might cause Andy to give up his own life altogether."

"Yes, Andy …" Annais said thoughtfully.

Twyjan looked at Annais quizzically. *Does Annais know who Andy is?* he thought.

"Yes, yes, of course," said Annais.

Never a dull moment, thought Twyjan.

"Okay, next question: Did you notice who was there?"

"Uh, me and David?" Twyjan felt silly as soon as he said it. "Oh, you mean, who took David?"

"Yes," Annais prompted.

"Well, it was someone quite tall, dark hair, menacing look. I only caught his profile, but I didn't like the looks of him." Twyjan seemed to shudder a bit just describing the guy.

"Hmmmm." Annais glanced to the picture above his desk and seemed to get lost in it for a second.

"Okay, that's enough for now," Annais said. "I need something else from you."

"Sure, anything," Twyjan said quickly.

Annais rose up from the coffee table and reached under Twyjan's armpits to pull him up.

"Come with me."

Still a bit wobbly, Twyjan kept in step with Annais over to what was the most decadent office desk he had ever seen.

Annais turned and said, "Wait, I need you to bring David's story."

Twyjan felt a pit in his stomach but did as he was told. When he picked the book up from the coffee table, he recounted the scene of losing David one last time. And he knew there was something he had forgotten. He stopped, looked at Annais across the room, and said, "There was someone else."

Annais stood deathly still and replied, "Do tell."

"I couldn't see him really well, because I was running at this point. But he was big. Like super-size, type big. And he had kind of this square head. He was the one holding David, while the other one was yelling at him." Just the memory made Twyjan feel weak again.

"Last question," said Annais.

Twyjan braced himself.

"Was he blond?"

What an odd question. But, well, he had been.

Twyjan said simply, "Yes, bright blond, and he was rather clumsy."

Annais seemed satisfied and turned back around.

Twyjan resumed his trek across the room, this time with the book in hand. He noticed Annais turning on a desk lamp. In the light of that lamp, he saw Annais adjusting some book ends. They were large golden bears, and they appeared to be almost protecting the books in between. Twyjan felt very reluctant to let go of the book in his hands.

He looked to Annais, whose hands were now out.

"You must trust me, Twyjan," he said.

And with that, Twyjan gave the book to Annais. He watched as Annais placed the book between two others. David could not make out the names on those books and briefly wondered if they were written in a different language. But he cared not. David's was there. And because of him, David was now gone. Twyjan wondered if this was a memorial bookshelf of sorts, all those who had been lost to the Legion. He tried to count but lost track as Annais had walked up and grasped his arm.

"This is no memorial," Annais said firmly. "We must return now. I need you to go to Tawly when you get back. You must remain with her at all times, unless you hear otherwise from me. Do you understand?" Annais sounded more stern than Twyjan had ever heard him.

Twyjan just nodded his head yes, and then he was back. At the lodge.

Annais

Annais stood behind his desk. Three things Twyjan had told him were new. It took him about ninety seconds to make up his mind. He picked up the black phone and waited for an answer.

"Yes, of course. I understand," Annais replied.

He listened patiently as the party on the other line carried on and on. And then he said in a matter-of-fact tone, "I can certainly wait until it is safe. But don't make me wait for long."

He hung up the phone. He would make use of this time, he figured. He started to scan the bookshelf where he had just placed David's story. He walked along and thumbed through the books. He was working. But no one would have guessed it. It appeared as if he were searching for something to strike his fancy. He walked along the bookshelf and then stopped and gazed at his painting. And then he began his survey work again. As he was deep in thought, his door blew open. He whirled around. It caught him off-guard, as very few people walked right into Annais's office. He was surprised, but when he saw who it was, he broke into a smile. He came out from behind his desk to greet his visitor.

The man who arrived looked disheveled and under duress. He was wearing street clothes and looked a bit like a gang member. He had a baseball cap on backwards and a leather backpack slung over his shoulder. Annais strode up to him and shook his hand.

"Thank you for coming on such short notice," he started.

"Quite honestly, it is my pleasure," the man said.

"I assume it has been difficult," Annais replied quickly. "I wish I didn't have to ask it of you. But alas …"

"Never mind," the man said, obviously interested in cutting to the chase.

Annais looked at him and then beckoned him to the couch. The man sat down and opened his backpack, and Annais grabbed some papers from his desk drawer. After discussing several issues for about an hour, they both packed up. The man looked at Annais before he stood up to leave.

After a moment of silence, he shook Annais's hand and said, "This one is for Tawly. This time, you will not be disappointed."

And he walked out the front door.

Tawly

Twyjan ambled over to the fireplace. Tawly happened to be sitting by the window, but he had not noticed her. She watched him closely, for now just happy that he was alive and home. She knew he was not physically injured, but he looked like he had been in a fight; he seemed broken down somehow. She wondered if the Legion had hurt him, but then she reminded herself that bodies could not be broken or permanently injured here. Rather, health seemed to flourish in the Next Place. No, Twyjan must be suffering something internally, she surmised. Her spirit, which had always been eerily in tune with those she met on earth, sensed that Twyjan just needed someone to talk to.

Twyjan's eyes darted around the room, as if he was unsure of the others here. Unlike on earth, where people often displayed a fake façade, the people here wore their hearts on their sleeves. Tawly sensed pain in Twyjan's searching look, emanating from his eyes. Tawly was reminded of the first time she had seen Twyjan. He had been immersed in that huge book, and the only thing she had seen was his wiry hair popping out atop the binding. Although he looked sort of crazy, the energy he gave off had been very grounding, very steady. And sure enough, as she had gotten to know him, this had proven true. Twyjan was dependable and trustworthy. Now, he had become her friend and somewhat of a mentor. And all she wanted was to know what had hurt him so. Why Annais had been summoned. And why something like this, whatever this was, could happen here.

His eyes locked with hers, and he nodded toward the fire. She nodded her head in agreement. Twyjan shuffled over and lowered himself into one of the cushy armchairs. Tawly walked over and sat gingerly beside him on the ledge of the brick fireplace. She wanted to embrace him and just hold him, but first, she wanted to listen to him. She looked at him expectantly, but not in a prodding manner. And she waited. Not one word passed between them for several minutes. And then Twyjan began. His eyes wandered out to the forest beyond the outside deck; his speech was barely audible.

"I failed Annais."

Those were his first words.

"I failed all of us," he then added.

"Oh, no, surely not!" Tawly rebuked the very idea, figuring that Twyjan was just being dramatic.

Twyjan reached out, touched her hand, and shook his head, saying, "Yes, Tawly. We do not win every single battle. This one, we lost."

The things Zaduk and Raynia had told her were swirling around in her head.

"Yes," Twyjan confirmed. "What they said was true. We lost someone. My someone. My David. That little boy was mine to take and to protect until he got here. We lost him. And it was all my fault."

Well, what in the world could that possibly mean? thought Tawly.

Twyjan took his eyes off the forest and turned so he could peer straight into Tawly's eyes.

"It means that the Legion captured him, and I was the one sent to protect him."

He looked at Tawly blankly and then continued, "I am haunted by the horror on his face after he was taken, his desperation. And I don't know what to do about it."

"Well, you were just with Annais, right? Surely he told you," Tawly said with a touch of indignation.

"Ah, no, Tawly. Annais is not responsible for that which the Legion inflicts on us. I think that there was a mention of some sort of retribution. That I should not lose heart, but ..."

Tawly interrupted him. "But what are you to do? I thought that Annais had all the answers. So what can you do?"

"Well-l-l," he stammered. Twyjan looked right at her and added, "He did comfort me, in a roundabout fashion. He also told me one last thing."

Tawly felt hopeful, until Twyjan spoke:

"He told me to come to you."

And then the hope drained right out of her. If Tawly wasn't confused before, now she was utterly confounded.

"Me? Are you sure you heard him right?" she asked, wanting to laugh but also wanting to cry.

Twyjan nodded his head and said, "With Annais, there is absolute certainty."

She knew this, of course. Twyjan shrugged his shoulders. And they both looked expectantly into each other's eyes for the solution to the riddle. Both searching, both returning to port empty-handed. Tawly sized Twyjan up. He seemed a bit better. Which was good. But Tawly thought she'd like to go run into the woods and live with the deer. Which would not be good, she concluded. There was no way she could fix whatever had happened. Annais must be wrong. There is a first for everything, she surmised.

Twyjan had spotted another Taker, someone Tawly had seen him hang out with before. So she smiled and got up to hug him, knowing he needed to talk to someone who understood. After a long hug, Twyjan pulled back from her and said, "I guess you're my new best friend. I'll see you first thing in the morning. Right here. For ... whatever."

Tawly did laugh. And once Twyjan was caught up in conversation with that other guy, she figured she couldn't make it another minute. She headed straight back to her room. She didn't even turn the lights on. She just went right for the bed. This day had been enough to make her want to pack her bags. For where, she had no clue. She quipped to herself, *Maybe there is a Third Place.* And then she was grateful she still had her sense of humor. Come to think of it, she had laughed quite a bit while she was here. This whole bit about her fixing things for Twyjan was no laughing matter, however. This seemed like an uber big mistake on Annais's part. Maybe she'd go see him tomorrow and tell him so. She would decide in the morning. She was taking off her thinking cap and putting on her night cap. She tucked herself under the covers and stretched her toes under the big down comforter.

When she did, she felt something altogether strange on her toe. It was a wet sensation. It tickled.

Hey, wait a minute, she thought. "Who let the dog in my bed?" she cried out.

Tawly jumped up, flipped on the reading lamp on her headboard, and threw back the comforter. Sure enough, there he was: a sleepy-eyed puppy. The little lab yawned and looked at her through his squinty eyes. He was almost smiling at her, she figured, and she just about fell off the bed in shock. *How could this be? I didn't even know there were dogs here,* Tawly thought. She tried to recall seeing any other dogs.

The puppy whined a little and shook his rear end, trying to get his tail moving. That was it; Tawly was taken. She crawled to the back of the bed and got her nose right close to him. It was there: the puppy smell. Tawly breathed it in heavily and then pulled back. She was having the sensation of déjà vu. Was that possible in the Next Place? Tawly was sure she was hallucinating now. This was all too much. Her mind started racing. She got a little closer to him. He snuggled his nose up under her chin. And then she knew for certain. There was no way. But there was no way it was not true. This was Scout. Scout had been that "one" dog for Tawly. She had loved many dogs in the First Place. But Scout had come along at a tumultuous time in her life. He had been saved after jumping out of a pickup truck on the highway that ran through town. He had survived the fall with three broken legs, but apparently the driver had not noticed or not cared, because no one had come back for him. So Tawly had taken every last penny she had and saved that dog. He had operations and medicines and rehab and long-term care. But for as much as she had saved him in those first months, he had saved her many times over in the years that would follow. She had called Scout her soul mate. And when he had died, just months after Janey had been born, a part of Tawly had died as well.

Could this really be Scout? He was little again. And, well … alive. Tawly stood up. And then she noticed a note tied around a royal blue collar on Scout's neck. Why was she calling him Scout? She must be nuts. She bent over and read:

"Do not worry. Love, Zaduk."

Oh, sure, thought Tawly. *Easy for you to say. You're not imagining that your old dog from the First Place has spontaneously come back to life and shown up in your bed in the Next Place.* Tawly felt like crying. But then under the note, she saw a gold gleaming pendant on the puppy's collar. Tawly got closer, and with that puppy panting in her face, she read the inscription aloud:

"SCOUT."

The puppy came bounding toward her. He had heard his name. She caught him before he flew off the bed and hugged him for the first time in decades.

13

Jane

I circled the rug in the living room. I kind of moved from one corner to the next. I was pretty sure I had gotten off the couch with the notion of getting dressed and with the less immediate goal of going to the grocery store. But that was a long-range, distant goal. Because just getting out of my mom's flannel pajama pants and the long john shirt, which I had bought to match, would be a big deal.

It would be a good first step to just change clothes, I thought to my floundering self.

But before I could embark on that earth-shattering task, in the middle of the rug, I stopped. A thought had just occurred to me: If I did manage to peel off this shirt, which had three days of my restless body sweat clinging to it. And if I was able to brush my teeth, which I figured I had maybe brushed at some point the day before. And if I could muster the strength to put my shoes on (of course, after I took off my cumbersome woolen socks). If I could get through all of that, then I would have to find thinner socks, maybe matching ones, in the mass of laundry that I had not put away in—well, a long time. Then there was the driveway, the snow to shovel, or I could just chance it and back out into the newly fallen snow—but first to get myself mittens, a hat, a coat, and a scarf. Well, maybe I would skip the scarf. I didn't like things around my neck these days. I had never felt panicky about choking until all of this had happened. Now, I choked almost daily. Whether it was on my own tears, or words, or just metaphorically gasping for my next breath. I always felt like I was choking. If not being strangled. I would let the frigid wind whip me in the neck instead. I barely felt it anyhow. But even if I could tackle every bit of it, what, pray tell, would happen if I made it to the grocery store? There was only one grocery store in this little town. The same one where I had had my meltdown.

"Meltdown? What a dumb word," I mused out loud to myself.

And then I remembered the meltdown happening: All of my resolve, all of my courage, all of my hope, all of my plans for life had melted into a pool around my feet, as I stood in that grocery store parking lot. On what was an otherwise, typical fall day, around noon, I had learned my marriage was doomed for good. Like nail in the coffin-type doomed. This was just days after my mom's funeral. I was looking back at myself in that big puddle of "what might have been" and saw the face of the girl who once was. It was me, yes. But on that day, if you saw me in that parking lot; well, I might have looked like I had been drained of my very spirit.

"Meltdown is the perfect word," I corrected myself in retrospect.

Now, in my living room, thinking about that fateful day at the grocery store, I recalled an article I had read about wildlife, which always grabbed my attention. And it had taken place in a town not too far from Fenton, which had also piqued my interest. The article told of a motorist cruising down one of the rural highways in central Michigan. The motorist had to slam on his brakes as a fawn had appeared in the middle of the road, seemingly from nowhere. Up until this point, this was a very typical story. But the rest of the article had hooked me: The author had fastidiously described what that event must have seemed like from the deer's perspective. The sound of the mad rubber tires screeching against the pavement. The scream of the horn, which was blaring out of the hood of the metal beast barreling down on her. The subsequent terror as she realized she had lost her herd, who had crossed the road ahead of her. And the resultant phenomenon: The little deer had been rendered completely immobile. Try as they might, not one of the people who had pulled off onto the side of the road, as the traffic had begun to back up, could coax that little deer to move. It took the act of one Michigan state trooper to finally get her to safety. He moved in slowly, picked the deer up by its torso, carefully wrapped her legs under his arms, and carried her to safety on the other side of the road.

Recalling this tragic story, I knew that the same force of nature that had shut that little deer down had done the same thing to me on that sorry day in the VG's grocery store parking lot. I had been utterly shocked by a monster which I could never have dreamed would come down the road for me. My people had crossed the road. And I was alone. And I could not move. I could not even find my way home. Ironically, in my immobility, I had reached for my mobile phone. I had texted the two people who had met me in my anguish so many times before: Elaina and Maggie. And after I sent them SOS texts, I stood there, hoping that a car wouldn't hit me. I had been, after all, standing smack-dab in the middle of a busy VG's parking lot.

The playback of this fateful day started to fade as I stood in the middle of the living room rug and recalled what I was trying to do. I reoriented myself to the present and stared out the window. It was gray outside. The kind of gray I figured only Michigan could boast about. It was one of those days where it seemed as if one big cloud might be covering the entire peninsula. I took notice but could not bring myself to care. Perhaps it was not possible to feel any more depressed. I briefly contemplated popping one more antidepressant to see if that would get me out the door. And then I shook that notion off. I had always thought of myself as the adventurous type. But there was one thing I was not: a rule breaker. If the doctor, the professor, the counselor, or even a recipe said so, I took it as gospel. And all of the above, in some form or fashion, made it clear: Do not mess with antidepressant dosages, unless you are looking for trouble. I flirted with the idea of wanting trouble and then let it pass. I would just go back and sit on the couch a bit longer. Surely something would move me.

I was in a trance of sorts. So when the gray Taurus pulled slowly into the driveway, against a backdrop of the gray atmosphere; I missed it entirely. Instead, it was the attack-dog-style barking of my otherwise rather docile Labradors that alerted me: My dad had just arrived. I felt relieved and simultaneously panicked.

What was he doing here?

How could I be kind?

How could I hold a conversation?

How could I care what he was feeling?

And then the obvious: How could I not?

Abaddon

After Abaddon had successfully ripped David from the Road of the Taken, he felt back in the zone. He was sort of super charged by David's heartbreak. He had heard him crying in the night and had gone over to Ike's tent, where he was being held, to rub some salt in the wound a time or two. And then he was ready for Jane again.

Perfect. Perfectly set up, thought Abaddon. *She will be like putty in my hands.* Abaddon had been lingering outside of Jane's house, watching her in her living room. He was unsure what she was doing, and he wasn't even sure if she was in her right mind as he watched her pace around the room. Honestly, he thought she might already be certifiably crazy. Even he, the snake that he was, might not feel comfortable knocking off a straight crazy person. He laughed a little at this possibility and then smiled in a cockeyed fashion. He began to recall some of his other victims, the ones he had driven to destruction before Jane. They had all exhibited some form of this temporary lunacy. He knew this to be true. It was evident in their eyes, a kind of wild-eyed gander they had, or it came down to crazy behavior like Jane's. Circling the living room rug like she thought the floor beyond the rug was the forbidden forest.

Gee, he thought. *She's not going to take too much convincing.*

So when Jane's dad pulled in, Abaddon said to himself with delight, *Surely I can wreak some havoc between these two.*

Abaddon watched Jane slowly answer the side door. He thought she might just implode by the panged look on her face. She muttered a form of salutation toward her dad and then ambled away from the door. Jane's dad let himself in with one hand as he held a grocery bag in the other. Abaddon scoffed at the show of concern and went to work. He had no way of knowing what Jane was thinking, but he was a veteran in these sorts of situations. *Shame might work nicely,* he thought. So he started in:

Look at that, Jane. Your poor widow of a father has to bring you groceries.

As if he doesn't have enough to deal with.

What happened to that great career you thought you had?

Now you have to rely on your old man to bring you food?

How about that? Saltine crackers for the crazy and destitute?

What use are you, anyhow?

You are not of any use any more.

You are USELESS.

USELESS.

USELESS.

USELESS.

Wait until little Gwin grows up and realizes her mom is a straight lunatic, a basket case.

Why don't you just give it up now so you don't have to answer that one?

The voice was screaming in Jane's head. Abaddon could sense it. She was clinging onto the kitchen cupboard, not hearing one word of her doting father. Abaddon knew it. He had her. And sure enough, Jane snapped. She spun on one foot, with a half-crazed look in her eyes, yelled at her dad for who knows what, and stalked to the back of the house, slamming the bedroom door behind her. Within seconds, her dad's car was pulling slowly out of the driveway, and Jane was hiding just inside her bedroom door. Abaddon figured that she wished she were dead already. He contemplated that maybe this second visit would be enough. Maybe he had overestimated Jane. He knew he had pushed her to the precipice. He almost wished it had not been so easy. Such a fleeting experience, he noted. It was just a matter of time now, he gloated to himself. And with that, Abaddon was gone.

14

Jane

I stood, weak-kneed and hollow chested, just inside the door to my bedroom. It was as if I was hiding from an intruder, but of course, I was the only one in the house. I thought someone would come around the corner at any moment and stab me right through the heart. This irrational thought was one last confirmation that I was looney. There was no other explanation for the verbal assault I had just endured. Except for the obvious: The voices kept coming because they were speaking the truth. I could no longer avoid it. I was just running away from what everyone else in the world knew to be true. When people looked at me, they thought these very same things. My dad thinks I am a failure; all those years he said he was so proud of me, he must have just been waiting for his pretender daughter to finally fall apart. And my husband and his new girlfriend. I knew they made fun of me. My sister: Well, she always thought I was kind of a pain. My friends: They just felt sorry for me and had gotten sick of listening to my drama, anyhow. There was no one who thought I was worth anything anymore. Well, there was Gwin; I stopped my tirade for one second. And then I reminded myself that she too was getting older. And she already looked at me kind of funny. Give her a couple years, and she would see right through my façade; she would hate me for it. That was it. It was true. I held no value to anyone anymore. Useless indeed.

I knew right then: I was done for. I was alone. Gwin was with her dad, most likely having the time of her life, since he was the party parent now. I could leave. No one would know the difference. It would alleviate them all. And I could go wherever my mom was. I hoped. I had to. I could not take it here anymore. Not one second.

The voice in my head reverberated:

You are USELESS.

USELESS.

USELESS.

USELESS.

The decision was made right then. In the final "useless," the decision was a new resolve. It was something to move toward. I would find some sort of medication that would put me to sleep. For good. Just like that. This made me feel a bit crazy in my mind and lost in my spirit, but at least I had a goal I could physically move toward. I had spent most of my life striving to reach goals. So very much. So this would be second nature. Plan. Prepare. Execute. At least I could feel good about following through with something.

It was as if I were watching from outside my body. I was visualizing what I needed to do. The same way I had reached so many goals before. See it. Then, do it. Get Gwin's favorite stuffed animals together and place them by the door; that way, when they got here, she would be distracted and someone else would find me. Then, to get the dogs in the basement. I did not want them to alert the neighbors. I wanted to make sure it had time to take effect. Then finally, to get to the cupboard and get something lethal.

I felt numb but I forged ahead. I found the ragged old bear that my mom had bought Gwin when she was just a few months old. Tootsie Bear was his name. I placed him on the front couch and put a couple of his pals around him. I found a half-inflated balloon in her room and took that with some tea cups and put them all together, as if they had something to celebrate. Even the stuffed animals would be happy I was going, I lamented. I petted each of the dogs before I let them downstairs. I even gave them a little extra food so they would be happy the last time they saw me. And then, I walked into the kitchen, opened the cupboard, and reached for a bottle of pills.

Tawly

Tawly arrived at Janey's in a jubilant mood. She had played with Scout for a good while before she passed out on her bed. She slept like a baby, though, and woke up just in time to meet Twyjan in the common room, as she had promised. Every morning, she looked forward to being able to see her daughter and her granddaughter. This time, she would get to show off her beloveds to her new best friend, Twyjan. The morning after Annais had told Twyjan to stick to Tawly, and Twyjan had relayed that back to Tawly, they had decided that she really needed to get back and check on Janey. In all the commotion of late, it had been a couple days since she had seen Janey, and she just couldn't wait to see how well she was now. Tawly figured Janey might be really gaining ground. And collectively, the two of them couldn't really come up with anything brilliant to do otherwise.

So Tawly had said to Twyjan, "Well, then ... let's go."

She barely noticed the remnant of Abaddon's recently departed presence. Tawly stepped right through the putrid air that hung on the doorstep and pulled Twyjan inside with her. It didn't take long to notice that the little house seemed subdued, however. Had Janey put little Gwin down for a nap? She noted the in-progress stuffed animal tea party. Where were they all? Perhaps Janey was getting some much-needed rest and respite herself? Tawly searched each room hopefully, with Twyjan on her heels. And then she stopped. She heard Janey before she saw her. It was a desperate sobbing sound. She knew this flavor of Janey's cry. It was that same one she cried when she was younger and had done something that had landed her in big trouble. The "I wish I had never ..." kind of cry.

And sure enough, coming around the corner, Tawly could hear Janey's desperate words underneath her cries: "I wish I had never been born. I never should have become a mom. I am never going to get better. I never want to have to look my dad in the face again. I never want to have to look another human in the face again. I'll never see her again. Never. Never. Never."

Janey sounded like a wounded, wild animal. Whatever was she wearing, Tawly thought, and then realized it was her old shawl. The one her daughter-in-law had knit for her to wear during the chilling chemo treatments. Tawly instantly wondered where Gwin might be. Surely, if Gwin were here, Janey wouldn't be howling like this? Tawly looked at Twyjan, who seemed bewildered. He looked back at her, and then they both stopped as they noticed something on the floor next to Janey: It was a bottle of pills, spilled about, next to a glass of water.

Tawly watched in horror as her daughter slumped down in her tears and fell onto the floor. Tawly did not even think it through. She just lunged for Janey. It was instinctual. She caught her in her arms and let her down to the floor slowly. Janey's eyes rolled back in her head and then closed. Tawly touched her chest to see if her heart was beating. She was taken aback by the warmth which spread up into her fingers, up her arms, across her chest, and seemingly right into her own heart. Was there an energy in Janey's cells that recognized the heart from which they had come?

Hogwash, thought Tawly. *I have a new body now.* Yet the mirth of the connectedness made all the logical thoughts disappear, and Tawly almost felt relieved. Until the next moment.

Jane

With the pills in one hand and my cell phone in the other, I walked back to the bedroom, took my mom's shawl off the headboard, and sat down. I had to send a couple of messages. It was not like me to do anything without some sort of written manifesto. So I began. I wanted to keep it casual, so as not to alarm anyone. They were already hyper-vigilant when it came to me right now. I was like a live wire,

I figured. They might even have certain scary ringtones to denote communication from me; who knew? First, my dad. I had to apologize. I couldn't leave with the words I had last uttered to him. Something about "just leave me alone." So I sent him a quick text, which he was just getting good at reading:

I am sorry, Dad. You know better than anyone how hard this all is. I wish I didn't take it out on you. Talk to you soon. Love you, Janey Bear.

I used my nickname from when I was little. I couldn't help it.

Then, on to my sister:

Hey, you. I just want you to know I am so glad you are doing well in your new place. Please tell the kids I say hi. I love you.

This felt empty, but she would know if I said too much. She knew me too well, even via the ubiquitous medium of texting. She always deciphered my mood. I had to leave it at that.

For Elaina:

Hi there, sister. Just wanted to thank you for all you have done for me these last few weeks. I might not have made it …

I stopped and erased the last sentence and continued instead with:

I sure have loved seeing so much of you lately, even under these circumstances. You are the best friend I could have ever dreamt up.

There, that was better.

Now for Maggie:

I just had to check in. I know how hard this has all been for you – still missing your dad – and then trying to console me. I see what you're going through and I just want you to know how brave and strong I think you are.

I thought about all the others, my cousins in Minnesota, my college roommate, my first two "work" friends from Chicago, all the little nieces and nephews (maybe not so little, but little to me), my aunts, my brother. Ugh. I couldn't take it. I started a quick message to my brother, and then the remorse began to set in, and the tears started to flow again. When the text message began to blur, each letter bleeding into a mire of pixels, my resolve to die began to blur as well.

How could I do this to all of them? I was already regretting walking to the cabinet, and the tears turned into the now familiar gasping and wailing. I was crying so hard that my chest seemed to be collapsing in on itself. The pills in my hand were the only thing I could see clearly any more. I had no idea how many I had started with, and I was trying to count them as they too began to look fuzzy. I was grasping for each breath, trying to puff air up into the area where my sternum seemed to be caving in. I was suffocating. I stood up, and the rest of the pills fell to the floor. And then everything went black.

As if on cue, each of my people started to flash in my mind. After all, it was all black to me, so each person's countenance had center stage to gaze right at me. They were clever enough to take turns, so that I had to be with them one on one. It was like a litany of exit interviews, but of the uber personal sort. At first, they arrived with that relaxed exhale-type look. And then their eyes and cheeks would sink a bit, questioning what I had just done, followed by a knitting together of their brows, which then fast-tracked to a desperate searching and poring stare. It was as if they had popped in to have tea, but were served up with an ugly cup of what I had done instead. Each one of them ended up with a look on their face that belonged distinctly to them and I. First, it was Maggie. Her parting look was one of hopeful anticipation, one that said "I am pretty sure you can make a better decision. I am just going to wait and see."

Well, the waiting is over, I thought in my panic. Wishing I could tell her I was sorry for my really, really bad decision, I thought of all the notes we had sent back and forth in the thirty-some years we had been friends. In seventh grade, during our fourth hour social studies class, she had sent me a short paragraph on spiral notebook paper, with swirlies and hearts on the outside, and inside it had gone something like this:

Jane,
I am not mad you for trying out for cheerleading, even though we pinky promised not to. I just wanted to stay with you at your house

on Thursday nights and now I might not be able to. Anyhow – want
to walk to the Library after school and then to the candy story?
I forgive you,
Maggie

Oh, now how I wish I could send her one more quick text. Certainly, our messages these days had evolved from those schoolgirl days. Now it was more along the lines of:

Hey –
Why didn't you call me last week? Busy?
Need to get together for coffee.
Stat.
Be there or be square.
Mag

But always, they had the same underlying message: You might do something wrong, but I will give you the benefit of the doubt and forget promptly because I love you that much. Given the gravity of what I had just done, though, I was pretty sure she was not going to forgive me.

This look of Maggie's stung. And there were more on deck.

My sister. I had borne each of the family's recent tragedies with her. The one person on the planet who could relate. And now I was leaving her. She was not the type that forgot. She looked sorely disappointed in me. And I was starting to miss her already.

My brother. He was in shock.

My father. He would be alone now. His eyes stared back at me with a lost expression.

Then Elaina showed up. She had always been the level-headed one. The one who spoke such reason and wisdom into my otherwise gypsy kind of a life: "What will Gwin do, Jane?" she said solemnly.

Oh, no, not Gwin. Please don't mention Gwin. And then Gwin's face showed up, replacing Elaina's stern stare. It was my baby with those soft, brown eyes. The ones that believed in me above all other humans. The one who had loved me to the moon and back 100 million times. The one who swore I would never know how much she loved me.

What.

Had.

I.

Done?

I had to look. I could not look away from her face. She was wearing that curious and questioning look that we shared. No one else quite got it. But it was a seeking look, a "Hi, I see you and wonder if you are okay?"-type question that we asked with our eyes. I wanted to mouth a reply. But it was too late. Her stare was the bottomless pit that I knew I could never climb out of. My chest was now laden with the lead weight of my decision. My throat constricted as every bit of my spirit seemed to be sucked right out. My eyes lowered into the low lands of my circumstance as my shoulders rolled forward into a surrender of my life.

The night Gwin had been born, there was a midsummer storm. We were living in Jacksonville, Florida, just off I-95 and within striking distance of the coastal thunderstorms. Weeks before little Gwin was to arrive, my husband and I had shoved the many tons of our accumulated lives into a U-Haul and had driven it down from Michigan to Florida. I had fretted over becoming a mom without my own within driving distance. Jacksonville was the closest city in Florida where we could make a living and still be within half a day's drive of my parents' retirement haven. They had retired to a little town called Briny Breezes on the west coast of Florida. It was a quaint little town, which many of the old timers lovingly referred to as Heaven's Waiting Room. My mom and dad had been the spring chickens of the group; none of the locals would have guessed that Iris's wait would end up being much shorter than their own.

And so, in a house freshly built, in a half-built neighborhood, my new reality was about to become absolutely concrete on that one summer's eve. It had started with indigestion. I had given up pop for the duration of Gwin's gestation. But that night, I had felt the urge to let loose a little. I had sucked down a full can of Sprite with my Chinese takeout. Five hours later, I had woken up with what I thought was a Sprite-induced tummy ache. I rose up from the bed to take some Pepto Bismol. When my husband had found me attempting standing push-ups against our faux fireplace to alleviate the indigestion, he said we needed to go to the hospital. In true Jane-like fashion, I had told him I would consult my pregnancy manual just to be sure. While my husband had searched deliberately for the hospital bag, I had searched through the pregnancy book's index. C ... for Contractions ... Yes, good thing I am so smart I had told myself. Page 194.. the last month.. contractions ... Aha! About thirty words into it, I had been convinced: I was about to have a baby.

"Honey!" I yelled. "We need to get to the hospital."

And there he had been, the big duffle bag in one hand and the car keys in the other. Ready, before the book had verified what he had already known.

When I had stepped out the door onto the welcome mat, I had sensed that a storm was unfolding. No rain had yet dotted our sidewalk, but the impregnated air had hung between me and the Jeep and had given a thickness to the dark night. On that drive to the hospital, besides the waves of pain, I had experienced a drifting sensation. There had been a pull on me that I could not define. The sky had been fettered with chain lighting as if it were a sentry, escorting us somewhere it knew of. It had been just us, my husband and I, in that heavy, gray-black night that was lit up by the lightning. It had felt like we were driving in a tunnel to somewhere. But I didn't know where.

In the rush of the move, I had not gotten the chance to take any birthing classes. My understanding of what was to come had been bound by what I had deciphered from books and from what other mothers had attempted to impart. I should have known then; the unspeakable act of creation could never be verbalized or taught. I was on the precipice of the single path to understand, to actually arrive at the door of creation. That was where the tunnel was taking me.

And now, in what I figured was the end of my life, as Gwin's face began to disappear, a similar drifting feeling had begun and the tunnel effect had followed. Oh, right, I had heard of this. People left the earth through a dark tunnel, right? That reminded me of something else I had heard: There must be a light at the end of this tunnel. I tried to open my eyes to search for that light. However, everything was pitch-black. But I was moving through the tunnel, I noted. And I was enjoying an incremental relief of weight. Was my body disappearing? I didn't remember hearing this was supposed to happen. I couldn't see my own body. But then I couldn't see anything at all. Was this my brain playing last-minute tricks on me?

And then this question seemed silly. I started to sense that it was more like the lifting of burdens. The weight of worry and grief seemed to be disappearing. There was a subtle settling in my thoughts. Doubts lifted off my shoulders, and the weight of so many questions with their gravitas effect floated off into a weightless space. I felt so light, so free. The darkness was diminishing. There was an undeniable lightening. Was this it? The light so many had spoken of? The one I had so simply pictured as the sunlight after a tunnel underground? I was so unencumbered. This felt like freedom, and I thought I could hang out here forever.

And then, like the night Gwin had been born, this trip through the dark tunnel ended. It was apparently just a doorway to a different place, a place I had never been before. Something felt very familiar here, and I couldn't believe it, but now there was a very bright light.

Tawly

Tawly found herself kneeling down in the middle of some gravel road. It looked familiar, but if it were, she had not been here in a while. She felt a heaviness in her arms and when she looked down at her daughter, she almost puked. Janey looked lifeless. And there was no one else here to do CPR, Tawly thought. Twyjan heard her thoughts and placed his hand on her shoulder from behind. He was so quiet.

Always in the shadows, Tawly thought now. But this time, he came right around in front of her and said in a stern tone, "Don't panic, Tawly."

"But what do you mean? Where are we?" Tawly asked in a hush, unsure why she was whispering.

"We are on the Road of the Taken; don't you recognize it?" Twyjan's eyes narrowed.

"Oh yes. Of course. Yes, I do. But why are we here?" Tawly asked as she surveyed the tree-lined path.

Then, she looked at her daughter's body in her own arms. She added two and two together. She had lost.

"Oh, no! It cannot be. Not my Janey. It wasn't her time. It wasn't supposed to be like this. I had other ways I was going to help her. There is so much more for her and Gwin and her friends and her life and ..." Tawly was running her words together now.

She was about to stand up and run the other way with Janey. She didn't know where to, but anywhere but here.

Twyjan clasped onto her wrist with one hand and shushed her with the other; he said, "Tawly, not yet. It is not over. Not yet."

"Whatever do you mean, Twyjan? I hate to say it, but denial is not going to work at this point. We are on the Road of Taken, this is my Loser, I am her Keeper, and that vile Destroyer Abaddon has won."

"No," Twyjan replied, not shouting but speaking more forcefully than Tawly had ever heard. "If Janey's time were up, her Taker would be here."

Tawly fought to think clearly in her panic.

"Well, what if you are here for her?" Tawly said. "What if that is why Annais sent you to stay with me?"

"No, no, Tawly, that is not how it works. There is a distinct Taker for those who are departing. And they never just land in the middle of the Road of the Taken. Something is amiss. And I don't think Janey is dead." Twyjan seemed certain.

Just then, Tawly felt the soft, warm exhale of a breath on her arm. In disbelief, she looked down as Janey's eyes looked up. It was as if they were back in Iris's hospital room, eyes locked, souls just settling in on the other. Tawly didn't know what to do. Janey answered by reaching up and grasping onto her mom's neck for a hug.

"The light," Janey said. "I just knew it was you."

"I have you now. Everything is going to be all right," Tawly said, with no clue how it would.

15

Abaddon

Abaddon was walking tall when he got back home. He figured he had finished Jane off with that last rant about how useless she was. Tomorrow, he would get a new assignment. So for tonight, he planned to revel in his victory. He sauntered up to the campfire and took a moment to survey the surroundings. He had not lived here the whole time. There were other camps. But he had made his way here when he had realized the proximity of it to the Road of the Taken. On occasion, he liked to wreak havoc on that road, as he had done with David a couple nights back. So this was convenient for Abaddon. He looked about and saw that the campsite was pretty desolate this evening. Not much life. But then, there was never much socializing within the Legion. Occasionally, you could hear a couple swapping stories or a few would get together to eat. But everyone stuck very much to themselves. And Abaddon figured that was how he liked it, anyhow. There were some embers in the campfire, but mostly just gray smoke. Abaddon decided he would head to his tent, which was not very well kept. Who had the time? he always reassured himself. If you were making your way to the top, you cared about one thing and one thing only: your next assignment.

Seemingly on cue, that idiot of an Assigner who had given Abaddon Jane walked into the clearing. Abaddon was feeling very proud of himself and was just waiting to hear him congratulate Abaddon that Jane had been taken. Destroyers always got notice from the Assigner when they had won. Of course, there was no party, because everyone was out for their own best interest here. No one would celebrate someone else's success. Abaddon could not even remember what comradery was like, but he didn't care. He knew that his fearless leader was aware how many Abaddon had destroyed. So when he saw this lowly Assigner, he sneered a bit with a hint of a smile. He couldn't for the life of him remember the guy's name. But Abaddon didn't really care to know anyone's name, certainly not someone as trivial as this guy.

Apparently, the Assigner didn't sense Abaddon's disdain, because he strode confidently over and said, "I want to congratulate you, Abaddon. Remember me? I am Ajax. How quickly you disposed of Jane."

Abaddon looked smug and ready for more.

Ajax continued, "Very impressive, but I do have to convey one small thing to you: There has been a wrinkle of sorts. Somehow, Jane has shown up on the Road of the Taken, not with her Taker, but with her Keeper ... oh, what's her name again?"

Abaddon's eyes narrowed, and he might have burned holes right into this guy with his menacing look as he said, "What exactly do you mean by a wrinkle, Ajax?"

Clearly a bit flustered, the Assigner spoke more quickly:

"Well, we knew you would be best to fix it. You are by far the most adept at finishing people off. We just need to bring her here. And then it will be done. You may even capture her Keeper at the same time. Perhaps this is your chance to exact revenge on her, as well."

With this, Abaddon confirmed what he had feared. This guy remembered that Tawly, then Iris, had gotten away from him so many decades before. Abaddon played a quick game of chess in his mind. He needed to be friends with this guy. Somehow, he wanted to ensure

Ajax forgot all of this. Maybe he would just do away with Ajax when he was finished with him. Abaddon thought for a second more: So it had been Ajax who had given Abaddon this assignment of Jane. Abaddon briefly wondered if the Legion's leader was toying with him. He shook that thought off and reassured himself. He was the best they had. It must have been this Ajax's way of trying to make an alliance with the much more powerful Abaddon.

"Okay," Abaddon said. "I will need someone to help me hold them. I'm not coming back without both of them. Let me go get my new apprentice."

With that, Abaddon changed direction and opened a small tent near the campfire. He grabbed David, who was sobbing on the floor of his tent, yanked him out of the tent, and slapped him to get him to shut up. Ajax wanted to help too. He beckoned to someone waiting in the shadows. Out came Ike.

Oh great, thought Abaddon. *Me and the Jolly Green Giant again. Oh well, maybe he can entertain this sniveling kid, and they can both learn a thing or two. And at least Ike doesn't speak much.*

Abaddon couldn't stand the drivel from most of the others he had to tolerate working with. Abaddon saw Ajax hand Ike something rolled up. Cash for stash, Abaddon thought. Ike would be drunk by midnight if everything went according to plan. Abaddon laughed out loud. A big loud laugh.

Ike just ambled up, looked right at Abaddon, and said, "Let's go."

Ah, just like the hired ox he is, thought Abaddon. He shot back, "Yes, indeed; let's go."

Abaddon hated follow-up work. He liked things to work out cleanly and as expected. He had been looking forward to a nice cigar he'd been saving up for just such a night. He was going to retire to his little place and end up with some good-smelling smoke billowing around him. Maybe even a short glass of whiskey next to him. He was not above these pleasures. But he doled them out to himself very sparingly. He would not be taken off the track he was riding to the top. Not by the pull of pleasure.

He started to recount the scene which he had left Jane in. Now, he had to see her pitiful face again. He hoped she was still crying, still wailing. That was all he hoped. He told Ike to make David walk ahead of him and to head for the Road of the Taken. Abaddon watched Ike sway back and forth through the brush, and again he began laughing. He couldn't seem to stop. Ever since he was little, Abaddon had laughed about everything. Even if something was deathly serious, he could only laugh. Fear, sadness, worry, loneliness: They all manifested in laughter for Abaddon. He had always known it was not natural. But he did not care. He figured it made him superior.

Tawly

Tawly was quite sure she had never felt this happy. Not in this place and not in the First Place. Not ever. She basked in it for a brief interlude and then looked up to see Twyjan. He didn't look so placid. Rather, he was glaring into the trees nearby and looked, well, scared. And then the joy seeped out as Tawly sensed what Twyjan had already: The Legion was there. And as much joy as she had in her arms, the dread started setting in to steal it. She looked back down at Janey, who had closed her eyes. *Oh good*, thought Tawly. *I certainly don't want her to think she is unsafe.*

But wasn't she just that? Her Janey was here, on the Road of the Taken, which was not exactly the Next Place and was not exactly the First Place. Was she dead? Was her life on earth over? Why on earth was Tawly with her, if so? And where was her Taker? Tawly briefly pictured some lazy Taker sitting around eating bonbons. She shook the thought from her head. She had not met anyone like that in her time here. She was sure that was not the case. She looked at the one friend she had come to trust: Twyjan. He was still peering into the forest. He turned now and communicated with her without speaking out loud. He wanted Tawly to get Janey up and to start moving. He was going to stay right where he was. Tawly needed to walk Janey toward the entrance to the Next Place. Tawly looked back at him and wanted to argue in her mind. She didn't want to think about the implications. If she took Janey through those gates, surely her life on earth would be over. Gwin would be abandoned, the rest of her family devastated again by loss. She just didn't want to believe it. But the evidence and the urgency of the present situation won out. She nudged Janey and started to pull her daughter to her feet. Janey seemed bewildered but trusted her mom and just wanted to hold her hand and be next to her. She clambered up and started shuffling slowly alongside Tawly. Twyjan nodded at Tawly over his shoulder and then started walking the opposite way on the road.

From everything Tawly had heard, this was a bad idea. The Road of the Taken was protected, but just like David, who had been wooed off by trickery, once you were off it, there was no telling what might happen. Tawly felt worried, but again, she trusted Twyjan. So she kept walking, albeit rather slowly. She couldn't help herself. She began to think about the First Place. What was going on there now? How had Janey gotten so desperate as to have taken her own life? Surely that was what had happened. Tawly recalled the pills and the sobs and the whole scene. Thankfully, little Gwin had been with her daddy. Gwin's dad had saved her from watching her mom die. Was Janey really dead, though? Tawly felt unsure of this. Yet Janey was here. Again, as was so often the case, Tawly felt like her thoughts were running around in circles. So she took a deep breath and kept walking. All seemed eerily silent. She turned to just double-check on Twyjan. What she saw stole that last deep breath.

Twyjan's outer coat was disappearing between two birch trees. He had not stayed behind on the road, as he had told her. Instead, he was headed into the forest. The burgundy wool flashed against those bright white trees, and then he was gone. Janey stopped alongside her, as Tawly was now frozen. Should she abandon her best friend to what she knew was the most dangerous place he could go? Or should she chance not getting Janey to the gates? Tawly felt completely torn. The indecision seemed to wrap itself around her throat and crush her ability to make a move. She was lost. Janey looked at her. She recognized something in her mom that she had battled with for the months since her mom had died: the indecision as to how to move forward. The grip of fear. Janey sensed that Tawly was deeply worried about her friend. She grasped her mom's hand, took a 90 degree turn, and began walking briskly right into the darkening forest, with no clue as to what lie in store. Tawly had been caught off-guard, and once they had crossed over, it was too late.

As they stepped into the foliage and entered the darkness together, Tawly started to think of all the things she longed to tell her daughter. She didn't know what was going to happen in here. Right now, she wanted to stop and tell Janey where they were. She wanted to tell her what it was like past the gates. She wanted to explain her Gathering Place. She wanted to introduce her to Raynia and Zaduk and all the others. She wanted to tell her to lose the old chemo shawl, to throw it off her shoulders and let go of all the memories of the sickness, to forget all those things, that it was all trivial by comparison. That the Next Place was a haven for those who had to leave the First Place and that that which comes in the Next Place was so much more than Janey might ever imagine. That the cloak of depression Janey was wearing right now was merely sapping her of the First Place experiences which would carry on to the Next Place. Depression and despair could not come with her to the Next Place, though, so she ought not dwell there. She had so very much to tell her. But would she ever get the chance?

Twyjan

When Twyjan made the decision to step off the Road of the Taken, he knew it was an all-or-nothing risk. Annais had always told them that they were perfectly safe, unless they chose to enter the Legion's territory. That was an entirely different story. But quite frankly, Twyjan was still so jarred from David being ripped away from him that he felt this animal-like instinct to run into those woods. He didn't care who was waiting for him. He wanted to be a distraction so that Janey and Tawly could make it to the gates safely. If he was lost forever in here, he did not care. He figured his last stand would be to save Janey from being stolen. If he could do that for his dear Tawly, then he was willing to live in whatever dark cave they threw him in.

As he stepped into the trees, he heard someone chuckling. It was an empty laugh laced with evil. He knew now what he had suspected when he was back on the trail with Tawly: The same guy who had taken David was in here. But now, Twyjan wondered if he was here alone. *What kind of maniac laughs by himself?* he thought.

The creepy laugh had halted him underneath a huge old pine tree. Twyjan looked up at it now and thought that there was beauty, even in here, where the Destroyers liked to hang out.

Twyjan searched for some stars through the overarching boughs of the old tree. *Just the North Star,* he thought. *Let me at least see it once.* He was sure he would be stuck in some dark cave for the rest of his life if caught by this group. But the sound of footsteps drew his gaze back down. Twyjan was absolutely still. The sound was very close. He quit breathing audibly. And he waited. The deer's eyes caught his first. He felt badly admitting it, but his first thought was whether the deer here were good or bad. He then felt silly. All the animals were good. All the time. Everywhere. This deer was here with a message for him:

"The Legion is here, there are three of them; they know where Janey is, and they are after her. Janey is not dead. But she will be if the Legion snatch her."

Twyjan knew most of this already but was glad to hear that Janey was not dead. If the Legion got a hold of her, though, not only would she be dead, but she would be lost forever. She would be separated from Gwin in the First Place and separated from her mom in the Next Place, assuming Tawly made it back. Twyjan had suspected this from the moment they appeared on the road, but he had been hesitant to tell Tawly. Instead, he had decided to take matters into his own hands. He looked at the deer with gratitude. And then the deer told him something he did not know:

"Tawly and Janey are in the forest."

Twyjan could not believe this. But the deer had disappeared before he could blink.

What was Tawly thinking? Twyjan was completely baffled now. He closed his eyes to concentrate. If the deer were right, he calculated, then following that creepy laugh was his best bet. The Legion knew where Janey was. So Twyjan was sticking to the plan. He was going to follow the laugh and see if he found them. Then, he would do whatever it took. They were not leaving with Janey.

When Twyjan had stepped into the forest, knowing that he might never be able to go back, he trusted Tawly would make it to the gates. He wondered if Tawly realized what kind of risk she was taking. Well, he could not figure that out now. First things first. He lent his ear to any hint of sound around him. Where had that laughter come from? Where was it now? Twyjan had been a Boy Scout in the First Place. And he was putting those skills to the test now. As an adult, he had started to think it was silly to have spent all those years becoming an Eagle Scout. Now he thought it was a stroke of genius. He decided to scale the old pine he was under and look about. Once he got twenty feet or so up, it was obvious to him that he had not gone very far. The Road of the Taken was in sight, and even the glow of the light beyond the gates was apparent, though dim. Twyjan began to scour the surrounding forest for movement.

16

Tawly

Tawly was moving with care through the forest; she felt like she could do anything with her Janey by her side. Yet she secretly hoped that she would not run into the Legion. The closest she had been was spotting Abaddon on the roof that one night back in her old neighborhood. The night Janey had "heard" her signing the lullaby. Tawly glanced over at Janey now … wanting to ask her about just that. But this wasn't the time or the place. So instead, she just grinned at Janey, and Janey returned the look, with a mischievous grin of her own. It was like they were in an unexpected adventure together, like life had been before Tawly got sick. So Tawly went back to trying to figure out what she would do if she ran into the Legion. And kept her eyes peeled for any sign whatsoever of Twyjan. She wanted to know Twyjan was okay. She put on her game face and got serious.

But the very next second, Tawly was sure she felt the ground shake. She stopped and put her finger to her lips to make sure Janey was quiet. They stood as still as the trees around them. The heavy footsteps were foreboding. Whomever it was, they were big. Tawly envisioned the gates now. She thought about just yanking Janey along and sprinting for the road to get to the gates. Janey must have sensed something though because she touched her mom's face and shook her head back and forth. *Could she read minds too?* Tawly mused. But then she remembered how well her Janey knew her. How Janey could just be in the same room and sense what was on Tawly's mind or in her heart. The corners of Tawly's mouth turned up, and her eyes softened at her daughter. As if to say okay.

Twyjan

Twyjan heard the laughter and spotted the branches of other trees swaying violently, as if some huge creature was pushing through the forest, perhaps a hundred yards from Twyjan. He looked down, calculating how quickly he could get down this tree, when a very familiar voice reached his ear. Twyjan froze. He would know that voice anywhere. It was his David. And then there was the voice of the vile man who had taken him. He was the one laughing. David was crying, kind of. And he was still talking about Andy. Twyjan's gut started wrenching again. He had been so busy with Tawly over these last couple of days that he had started to move past the immediacy of the anguish he had felt over David. But now, it was back. Like an unexpected visitor. He was completely unsuspecting. This caught him by surprise, and all he could do was listen and watch. They were practically underneath him now. And he could see them. There were three, just as the deer had told him. Twyjan quickly recognized the tall blond as the one who had held David when he was stolen. And the creep in the back was still laughing as David seemed to wail on.

Suddenly, the tall one broke stride. Abaddon yelled ahead to tell Ike to stop. And when David turned around to see what they were going to do next, he started in:

"You are such a weak, worthless child, David. I should have never taken you. I thought you would be an asset to our team. I thought I could count on you to walk into my shoes, to become the best of the best. I even considered the idea that you might be my prodigy. That you could walk alongside me and learn all that I have to offer a young one like yourself. Too bad ..."

As his voice trailed off, David looked at him and said, "But you lied to me. You told me that you would help me save my big brother," his voice crestfallen and throaty from all of the crying.

Abaddon threw his hands up in an act of surrender and said, "David, it is time to grow up. It is time to face reality. There is no one who needs you back in the First Place. I could show you. Their lives go on. Yours is over there. You only have what is here now. That moron of a Taker was just tricking you. There is nothing worthwhile in the Next Place. They don't even have the chance to gain the power and prestige that you will have here. The only thing that matters is here." Abaddon pointed at the ground. "And now. And you. You will choose for yourself what you get. There is nothing else, only what you see. If you don't listen to me, you will forever grovel over people who no longer even care about you."

These last words stung David. Andy had once told him, "Mom and Dad no longer care about us."

David had thought that was the craziest thing he had ever heard. But maybe this guy was right. He was certainly convincing. He noticed Ike was giving him a strange look. And the Destroyer was just looking like he could not stand one more minute.

Twyjan could not believe his ears. This guy was single-handedly undoing the things David believed in. Twyjan already despised the guy, but now he wanted to strangle him with his bare hands. He had stolen David from Twyjan, and now he was destroying his very spirit. Twyjan was ready. He began to crawl down the tree.

But just as he lowered his foot to the next branch, he heard Ike yell, "There they are!"

Twyjan froze. Ike took off. The Destroyer pushed David forward and then sprinted behind. Once they were out of earshot, Twyjan made his way deftly down and chased after them as fast as he could. He saw commotion up ahead. He could see the golden glow of Tawly, and her daughter was already in Ike's grasp. The Destroyer was striding toward Tawly, who was trying to pull Janey out of Ike's grasp. Twyjan did the one thing he could think of: He ran up behind David and grabbed him. David cried out. The Destroyer turned on his heels and locked eyes with Twyjan. Twyjan could not believe how scary this guy looked up close. Tawly could not believe that Twyjan was here. For a second, everyone was still. And then David wrangled around to look his captor in the face.

"It's you!" he cried, jubilant. And then almost instantaneously, he grew mad. "You lied to me."

"No, of course I did not lie to you, David. Why would I? There is no reason for me to lie to you. Think about it. There was more to tell, if I had just had the time," Twyjan said as he pulled back and let David out of his grasp.

The Destroyer started over toward them. He grabbed David and slapped him across the face.

"Believe that and you are a bigger idiot than I thought," he said, seething.

David shrunk. Twyjan sized up this guy's strength and knew he was outmanned. What could he do? he wondered. Tawly started to panic, keeping her eye on Janey in the circle of Ike's huge muscular arms.

Ike

In the days after David's capture, Ike had stayed in his tent, ruminating. No one had noticed that he hadn't come to the campfire to do shots at midnight. Or that he had missed out on the hangover discussions around the canteen the next morning. No one seemed to care that he was absent for his normal duties. He usually helped move supplies into the camp. It took someone strong and burly, and he was all that. What people didn't know was that under all that bulk and muscle, Ike had a bit of a soft spot. Not for just anyone. And certainly this place had all but hardened it. Yet something in that boy's eyes had stirred Ike. That David. That boy had taken a toll on the hard veneer he had built up. That night, when he had seen David's eyes searching for Twyjan, he had felt a deep welling up of something. But he had to force it back down. He had needed that whiskey, and he had been out. He couldn't imagine defying Abaddon anyhow. No one messed with Abaddon. So he had held on tight to David and forced him ahead on the path.

All the while, though, he had been wrestling with something on the inside that was telling him to let David go. At the time, he had told himself he was just experiencing withdrawal symptoms, which the whiskey would cure. He had not felt anything close to emotion in years, and certainly this silly kid wasn't going to change that. He had closed down the feelings and moved ahead with his orders. He had handed the kid off to Abaddon, took the cash he was promised, and headed straight to the trading place. That fifth of the best whiskey they had to offer was a reward, and he had retired with his newly won prize to his tent. He hadn't been feeling so social on that particular night.

In the days after they had seized David, Ike could not drink enough. That stupid kid kept popping into his head. And to boot, the kid's tent was just a stone's throw away. If Ike wasn't thinking about David, he was listening to him cry. He had lain awake at night, tossing and turning. There was something in that kid's eyes, but he had yet to put his finger on it.

What's wrong with me? he had chided himself. *Why do I give a rip about this kid?* He figured this kid might drive him crazy and decided to leave camp for a while; he packed up his bag for a night or two by the cliffs, but as he was walking out of camp, Ajax approached him and said that Abaddon needed him again.

"Just wait here," Ajax had said. "I have to tell Abaddon I found you."

Ike had shrugged his shoulders. He had thrown his stuff back in his tent and started dreaming up what he might drink to get him through another night in camp. He had a few things under his pillow, but it would be a tough one, no matter what. Something about Abaddon was hard to shake.

Now, as Ike stood in the clearing holding onto Janey, he glanced over at Twyjan and David. David looked so small and vulnerable.

143

Finally, it hit him: David was the kid he had been before the fame and before the drink. Ike had risen to stardom so quickly that he had stayed a child emotionally. He had never had the chance to mature. He had been like the little innocent child that David was now. Ike had been stolen from his chance at life too early. Not by an oncoming car, like David, but rather by the more elusive captor: alcohol. That's what it was. Ike had been lamenting his very own life this whole time. He had been wishing for the time he had wasted away in the First Place, before he had essentially killed himself with the poison in the bottle. He had seen the love David had for his family back in the First Place, and it had touched on the very things Ike had left behind. Ike's family had stuck by him even when it had become evident he had a drinking problem. Even when the headlines had accused him of drunk driving after his games and had said he was on a downhill slide. His parents had still been on his team. Always waiting for him to come home. Still, he had squandered it all. Slowly, yes. But still willingly. And this boy, this David. It was not his choice. He had been robbed. And Ike could not bear it. He looked over at David and noticed that Twyjan did have him, but was almost hugging him. Ike figured that Twyjan would try to stand up to Abaddon to save David. But Ike was a player. He knew who would win. It would be no contest. Twyjan was just not fit to battle the seasoned Abaddon. It wouldn't take long for him and Ike to clean up this whole motley crew. He could see Abaddon nodding at him now. He was glaring at Ike. Telling him in not so many words to go get David and that weakling, Twyjan. Ike nodded his head. He would go get them.

But on his way, he would say one thing. He had to. It came out as a whisper: "Annais."

17

Abaddon

Abaddon was busy wrestling Tawly's arms behind her back so that he could push her to lead the way back to the camp. He was so caught up in telling her how weak she was and how she had just ruined her whole family's lives, that he did not notice Annais's arrival. Abaddon pivoted around when he heard a big voice behind him. He was flabbergasted. It took him a few seconds, but he was certain just from looking at the guy. This was the storied leader from the Next Place. Annais was here. How could that be though? Abaddon was wracking his brain. Annais was not allowed in the forest unless someone who lived there summoned him. This made no sense. Abaddon's head was spinning. As he lost his sense of control everyone else stood deathly still.

Annais had anticipated this. In fact, he had quite set it up. When he arrived they were all there. Everyone he had planned for. He strode up to Abaddon and easily unhanded Tawly from his grip. Annais then motioned to Ike, who much to Abaddon's chagrin, walked casually over as if he and Annais were old friends. Annais winked at him as he approached. Lastly, he looked at Twyjan and David and gave one of his very characteristic all face smiles. And then he motioned for them all to leave the trail toward the Road of the Taken.

Abaddon didn't move a muscle. He was in shock. No doubt. He had never set eyes on Annais. He was like a fairy tale to Abaddon. He had heard rumors about his stature, his smile, his thick wavy hair, and on and on. He couldn't take his eyes off him. There was something magnetic about him, Abaddon noted. He was kind of caught up in looking at him. On the other hand, Annais had seen the likes of Abaddon more times than he cared to admit. But for now, Annais was not taking his eyes off Abaddon either. In utter silence, the whole party filed into a line and began to walk out of the clearing. Janey was walking but was looking at Annais the whole while. Annais watched them all leave out of the corner of his eye and then his full attention was on Abaddon. He simply looked at him. Abaddon squirmed under the gaze. And even felt an impulse to barrel right into Annais. But he knew there was no chance. He attempted to stare back. But Annais was downright intimidating and Abaddon would have to look away. He would look at the ground and then would get the courage to look back up in defiance. For what seemed like an eternity, Annais spoke not. Until he knew the others had reached the road and were far from ear shot. And then he said:

"You have underestimated me once again. And fooled yourself right into defeat, Abaddon. I have watched you do this twice. I should like to think you might give up," Annais offered.

Abaddon could not believe his ears. He seethed back:

"Nah. Not a chance. You'll see how useless they all are in time. I have no need for any of them. I need no one. And I will never give up."

"The offer stands," Annais said as he gave one last thoughtful look at Abaddon. "You haven't much time though."

And with that, he was gone.

"What did that mean?" Abaddon shouted at the top of his lungs to no one. "You don't know me. You have no idea what I will do!"

He stood in the clearing in the middle of the dark forest in silence for a long time. And then, in true Abaddon fashion, he did the one thing that he had done since his mom had died: He started plotting his next move. He would go straight back to that loser of an Assigner and tell him that when little Gwin's name came up, he wanted that assignment. That was it. He would get his revenge. He didn't care about Annais and his stupid little stunt. He just hadn't seen it coming. This must be someone else's fault. He made all these conclusions quickly. He wanted to find that menial Ajax and interrogate him about the "wrinkle" with Janey. Then he would find a way to threaten Ajax to ensure no one else found out about this. Abaddon started walking briskly back toward camp. It would be easy to find him, Abaddon figured. No one else in camp wore a stupid baseball cap nor carried a silly leather backpack. He snickered to himself and as he walked he dreamt up his revenge on little Gwin and started laughing. Yet one question was lingering in the back of his mind, whatsoever had Annais meant about "not much time"?

Twyjan

Twyjan had gotten nonverbal instructions from Annais when he was smiling at him in the clearing:

Get to the road.

Get to the gates.

Go to my office.

So as soon as they made it to the road, Twyjan urged them all to move quickly. He was taking up the rear this time. Never again would he make the mistake of taking his eyes off anyone. They all listened and began to run toward the gates. Janey was first, for some reason, and seemed to know just what she needed to do. Tawly was on her heels, David next, and then the rather stout Ike was running with an uncanny ease as well. Twyjan sensed an energy coming from Ike that he had not felt from the meathead-like character who had stolen David before his very eyes. He cared not what had happened before. If Annais was sending Ike to the Next Place, then Ike belonged there. Twyjan's job was only to follow orders. They crossed the gates in a couple minutes, and as Twyjan caught up with them, he stopped to catch his breath.

And then he spoke just a couple of words: "Follow me. There is work yet to be done."

They all gathered near Twyjan, and in an instant, they were in Annais's office. This was the same place where Twyjan had woken up a couple nights prior. Everyone seemed uncertain as to what to do, so Twyjan led them over to the couches by the fire. He showed Tawly where the coffee and tea were, assuming she would serve the group. And then Twyjan stood by the windows, waiting for Annais.

As he watched, he noticed someone approaching along the road. And then he realized it was not one person but two. This alarmed him a bit. He knew he was safe here, so he stood and watched as the two figures became more apparent.

One was tall and lanky and had a long stride, and the other seemed bulky and muscular, a tad shorter with a quick measured gait. They appeared to be in intense back-and-forth conversation, and they were almost at the door before they noticed Twyjan at the window. When they did, both broke into big smiles and stopped. They seemed to be taking stock of Twyjan and then moved to the door and rang the doorbell, Twyjan thought. He opened the door and began to explain that Annais was not there. But the two men stepped right in and seemed to ignore his uncertainty completely. The muscular one put his arms around Twyjan, buried him in his chest, and then passed him off to the other guy. Twyjan wondered why he was being slapped on the back and smiled at.

"Don't worry," the strong one said. "We know Annais is not here yet."

"Well, how do you know that?" Twyjan asked, surprised. "Annais was just with us."

The two men looked at each other and then looked back at Twyjan and shrugged their shoulders.

"A different story for a different time," the burly one answered. "And by the way, my name is Xander."

Twyjan's manners kicked in, and he began, "Well, pleased to meet you. My name is …"

The other one cut him off short: "Yes, yes, we know, Twyjan. Let's cut past the formalities. My name is Asriel. We came right away because we just could not wait to hear the story."

"What story?" Twyjan now seemed a bit off-kilter.

"Well, the story of how you all beat that vile Abaddon, of course."

Twyjan had to stop. This had caught him entirely off-guard. He had no idea that the tall dark, creepy guy who had stolen David to begin with was the same exact Destroyer that Tawly had been battling. He looked over at the group and at Tawly specifically. She was smiling and talking to her daughter, positively lit up. He couldn't bother her with wondering how they had missed this right now. Perhaps later back at the lodge, over coffee. Twyjan was perplexed at how this had all unfolded. How could he have ended up in the final battle between Tawly and Abaddon and ...

"Now, that is not always for you to understand," Asriel said, smiling at Twyjan.

Twyjan sensed that these guys were somehow involved in what was feeling a bit like a setup.

"No matter," Xander said rather insistently. "Let's hear about how it all happened."

They were like little kids in a candy store, Twyjan thought.

"Indeed," Xander said. "We just love to hear the stories. It's our favorite part."

Twyjan didn't know what else to do, so he took them over to the couches. The two served themselves, one tea and one coffee, and listened like it was story time as the group talked about what had led up to where they were now. Ike seemed completely at ease, and David sat quite close to him when Twyjan wasn't by his side. Janey seemed altogether entranced by their stories and shook her head a lot when they spoke of things she did not understand. They all seemed to be in a bit of a dreamy fog, laughing and carrying on, when a door slammed in the back of the house. Twyjan had forgotten that they were waiting on Annais. He strode around the corner and stopped to look at them all. If Twyjan was reading Annais right, he had a great sense of pride in all of them.

Annais greeted everyone and made sure they had all been introduced. But it was back to business quickly. He told Xander, Ike, and David to come with him. They all jumped up and started to follow Annais to a door at the back of the office.

"Ah, but wait," Annais said in midstride. He turned back to the group and said, "Twyjan, please retrieve David's book from behind my desk. Asriel will show you what to do next. Oh, and Ike's as well, of course."

With this, Annais placed his arm around Ike's shoulder. This was the first time he had been able to embrace him in any way. He walked with Ike like this, and David grabbed onto Ike's hand. He had saved him, after all. Xander walked in front of them and seemed to be in the lead. They didn't know it yet, but there was some debriefing to be done. Annais and Xander would sort out some of the nonsense the Legion had poisoned these two with first. Then, they would each go on to a Mender in their own Gathering Place. It was their rite of passage, which they had both been previously denied.

Annais looked over his shoulder and winked at Twyjan, who was watching the four of them somewhat wistfully. David turned around and ran back to hug Twyjan. The whole room's spirits lifted, watching these two embrace. And then it was over. Asriel strode up next to Twyjan to help him, and the other four left the office. It would take them a minute to find Ike's story in the huge collection of books behind Annais's desk. Twyjan had not realized just how many were there. He wondered how Annais kept track and then shrugged the thought of. Annais knew, and that was enough for Twyjan to know. Asriel ended up finding Ike's book and handed it to Twyjan. Twyjan knew right where David's was, as he had watched Annais place it there just days ago. With both books in his hands, he looked to Asriel to show he was ready. Twyjan took one last glance at Tawly and her daughter. He knew he would see Tawly soon. But he didn't know when he would see Janey again. He watched her smiling with her mom, and rather than interrupt the joy, he said he was ready. They walked out the back door as well.

Jane

I was alone with my mom. I did not know where I was, but I was with her. I felt sensations coursing through my body of what it felt like to be in her presence. The light from the fire seemed to add to this unbelievable golden glow she had. *Where was here, anyhow?* I thought. But the thought came and went. Nothing mattered to me now. I felt the weightlessness I had been longing for over the last months: the freedom from the grief, the safety of her nearness. I didn't feel like I wanted to puke out my intestines, and I didn't have a hole in place of my heart. I was just so happy. She was looking back at me, and I knew she felt the same way.

Before I could even take it all in, I knew it was going to end. It was the look on her face.

"You cannot stay here, Janey," were the words she said, and I knew she was going to say them.

"But ..." I started in. And then I looked at her expression and didn't finish.

She had assumed the role as my mom one last time and was telling me straight. I was not to argue. Instead, I just looked at her and waited. Annais would come back; somehow, I knew this too. As I looked at my mom's countenance, I saw everything I had seen in the First Place: the larger-than-life eyes, which were a periwinkle I'd never seen before nor since; the perfect nose; the shiny blonde hair, which almost sparkled now in this golden aura she seemed to have; the twinkle in her eye when she looked back at me; the smile, which changed her whole face; the way she got thoughtful as she was about to tell me something; the way she looked over when she knew Annais was approaching. And the dread I felt between us. It was kind of like back at the hospital, yet here, it felt less desperate, somehow. I could not explain it, but seeing my mom here ... I just knew. It was all going to turn out okay.

As I told myself this, tears started to accumulate, and my eyes were suddenly pools of emotion. I could still see her, but now she was blurry. She reached for me and held onto my wrists. I looked down at her hands. They too were exactly as I remembered, but for a scar that seemed missing now. I thought to ask her, but then Annais was there. He had casually walked over to his desk, grabbed something, and then walked over to us. He smelled like the outdoors, I thought. Then he nodded to my mom, and she started to get up. I looked up desperately, and she pulled me up with her. She wrapped her arms around me and then held my face in her hands. I could have stood there forever. I would have. But Annais said she must go to the Grand Library now, and he handed her a book. I could have sworn it had my name written across the front, but how weird would that have been, so I shook the thought from my mind. She held that book under one arm and reached for me one more time, this time hugging my neck.

She kissed my forehead and told me, "Please kiss little Gwin for me. I love you, Janey."

I couldn't think of one thing, except, "I'll see you soon, Mom."

She nodded in agreement. And then she was gone.

Again.

I couldn't move. I had watched her walk out the back door; apparently, the Grand Library was somewhere else entirely. I had no idea. The only Grand Library I could think of was like a presidential library or something. But this sounded a bit more important than that even.

"I'll show it to you someday," I heard Annais quip.

I had forgotten he was even there. I looked at him now. And even though he had just sent my mom away from me, I somehow felt a very deep affection for him. When he had shown up in the forest, I had been shocked. I had thought he was the most fascinating man I had ever seen. He had a presence like no one I had ever met and yet gave off this super-casual vibe. I had wondered how he could seem so calm in the middle of such chaos. I had thought he might break out a gun or a sword, or whatever they fought with here. But instead, his words were the only thing he needed. He was mysterious and handsome and sort of like Mr. Rogers, all in one. I was definitely dreaming. Had to be, now that I thought about it.

"Not so easy," Annais replied.

Wait. I had not said anything out loud.

"Not really necessary," he said then.

"This is all so different," was all I could come up with.

Then he started laughing. This guy was unpredictable. One second, he was reading my mind; the next, he was having a chuckle with me. I felt a bit thrown.

"Ah, well. I have to keep you on your toes." Annais's eyes gleamed in the firelight as he said this.

"Yes, but did you have to take my mom away?" I blurted out.

"I was waiting for just this question. Come with me, Janey. I have much to tell you."

Annais held out his hand for me to grab onto. I didn't know where we were going. Nor could I have ever guessed.

Tawly

Asriel greeted Tawly at the door, which surprised her.

"You didn't know I was the librarian?" He grinned as he asked her the obvious.

"No, I didn't even know there was a Grand Library," Tawly replied as she peered into the monstrous lobby.

"Well, now you shall have the tour." And with that, Asriel closed the door behind them and nodded for Tawly to follow him.

He paused, glanced at her arm, and said, "You have brought your Janey's book, correct?"

"Yes, of course." Tawly was guarding the book with her life.

She knew not why, but for now, it seemed all she had of her

daughter. She didn't know if Annais had sent Janey back yet or not, but when he had returned and walked up to them at the fireplace, he had told Tawly (without speaking, of course), that he would be taking Jane back to the First Place and that she was safe now. Tawly had won.

Of course, she had walked away with mixed emotion. She had won, but it didn't feel like much of a prize. She knew it was best for the people back in the First Place, but it had been so nice to have Janey here. And then she remembered Gwin. And she knew that Janey must go back. She was going to be here eventually, Tawly had told herself.

"Good. You do realize that the Grand Library is where all the stories are kept, correct?"

Tawly nodded tentatively.

"I have the ones which are currently being written and the ones that are finished."

Tawly gave him a questioning look.

"I just keep them in separate wings," Asriel said with a wink. "We must keep things in good order. Correct?"

What was it with this guy and his obsession with correctness? Tawly chuckled in her head and replied,

"Correct."

All Tawly knew was that this was a much better place than behind Annais' desk. She had at the least figured out that those who were in peril of some sort, wherever they were, those were the stories sitting behind Annais's desk. Tawly hoped Janey's book was never back there again. She thought to ask Asriel. He seemed to know everything. Maybe he could just tell her if Janey was safe until it was her time. Maybe ...

But Asriel read minds too, which she should have bet on. And he interrupted her thoughts with:

"I certainly cannot tell you that. I am sorry. I am not even able. There is no such thing as a fortune teller here, Tawly. Unfortunately." He laughed at his own play on words.

He's kinda dorky, Tawly thought, *but in a cute way.*

Asriel had reached the circulation desk and turned at this last thought of Tawly's. He gave her a funny face and then launched into a full-fledged speech about the Grand Library. He was not kidding about a tour; Tawly laughed and leaned against the nearest card catalogue to listen to this incredibly intelligent man describe the inner workings of this awesome library. As he talked, Tawly admired the building itself. It was the most ostentatious thing she had seen in the Next Place. It seemed like no expense was spared. It must have been several stories high. She could not tell, as they were just on the first floor, but Asriel talked about it as if it went on forever. As far as her eye could see, there were stacks and stacks and stacks of books. Tawly was listening, but Asriel faded in and out as she was in a fog from the day's events.

When he was done, he told Tawly to follow him, and he marched down a path that seemed like a mile long. He looked up and down in the middle of what felt like one endless row and then said, "Ah, yes. Right here."

He pointed, and Tawly saw that indeed there was an opening that looked as if Janey's book might fit nicely in.

She hesitated and then looked at Asriel. For all of his rambling about his library, just now, he looked incredibly serious.

"Annais took very good care of Janey while she was in danger, sweet Tawly. But I am even more watchful than he. That much I can promise you." He paused and then added with a wink, "Don't tell him I said that."

Tawly believed him; and she placed the book where he said it belonged.

Jane

The first conscious thought I had was that my bed had gotten really stiff. I tried to open my eyes and struggled; they seemed to be swollen shut. Once they opened, I noticed the light pink pills strewn everywhere. And then it dawned on me.

What I had done.

What had I done?

I was unsure at this point. I started to piece it all together. I pushed myself up from the wood floor. I had curled up next to my bed. The dogs were whining from the basement. Apparently, they heard me stirring. They began barking. My head was pounding. Puffy. The way you wake up after binge drinking (or apparently binge pilling).

I didn't know how many I had taken. *Apparently not enough*, I thought. And then I laughed.

Why was I laughing? I should be livid at myself for my newest failure. But something felt different. What was it? And then that feeling hit me. The one of having been with my mom. That feeling started to saturate my senses. I was experiencing it all over. I could remember my face in her hands. I could remember her lips on my forehead. I could see her reassuring stare when she agreed I would see her again. Her laughter rang in my ears. The recollection of her smile started one in me. It was all at once. And it was positively sublime.

But how? Had I died and visited her? I started to remember a floating sensation. Ah yes, I must have died. Well, but why was I back here surrounded by spilled antidepressants and my cute, but rather irritating dogs? Certainly, I had not died and arrived back here. That would be a cruel joke indeed. Again, I laughed out loud. And surprised myself again. I took a quick inventory. Had I even laughed since my mom had died? I could not recall one single time. And in just five minutes, in the middle of my bedroom floor, with swollen eyes, and a huge crick in my neck, I had cracked up twice. For no apparent reason. This was good. I didn't understand it. But it was good.

Back to the floating sensation. Yes, I could remember that. And then a dark tunnel I was floating in. And then the light. No, a lightening? Ugh, I couldn't be sure. But it had felt so good. And then. Yes, then, I had opened my eyes, and my mom's face was all I could see. I was in her arms. I was with my mom. And then, well, there was nothing else ... except for being in some ultra beautiful living room of some sort. In the most astounding surroundings. There were trees blowing outside open windows and scents of gardenia and lilacs floating in on the warm breeze, and the smell of a fire that was putting off warmth. And the two cups of coffee that we sipped on as we talked. We must have been completely alone because I could not remember one other person. Was that where my mom was living now? Wait, she wasn't living. Was that where she was hiding? I laughed again. Who knew? All I knew was that she had held me. She had looked at me. She had seen me. She had told me to kiss Gwin. Ah, Gwin! My baby girl. Yes, I looked out the window. It appeared to be early in the day. Today was Sunday, if I had not lain there for more than one night. And Gwin should be home around noon. I needed to get myself together. I felt so happy she was coming home. I could barely stand it.

I was going to kiss her for her Mamie. I was going to share my mom's embrace with little Gwin. Yes. That was it. I started to get up and noticed my phone blinking. *Uh-oh*, I thought. All those text messages. I didn't even want to pick it up. I was petrified that I had said something too stupid, that someone might have called me out on my idiotic, mega drama.

Tawly

Tawly showed up on the deck of the Gathering Place. She had taken a heaviness with her upon departing the Grand Library. Not only did she want to stay with Janey's story and ask Asriel a couple more questions, she also hated being away from Annais. After being with him, she felt his absence profoundly. She figured it was time for a good, bold cup of coffee to go along with her jolt of reality. When she slid through the doorway into the common room, though, she was met with such a scene. It seemed everyone she cared for in the Next Place was there. Twyjan was standing at the front of the group, with exactly what she was hoping for: a steaming cup of java, in her favorite mug; she assumed it was a nice bold brew. Oh, how she had come to adore this quirky guy. He looked at her in his knowing way. He knew that

Tawly had just left her daughter. He knew that she had just finished her mission. He knew that she had just left Annais. And he knew that she'd had to leave Janey's story behind. It was Janey's to finish now, and Tawly would not be so intimately involved. Twyjan knew that the unknown was what was in front of Tawly. But he also knew that he would be there with her. Somehow, they had saved both of their protected ones together. And finally, he knew that she needed him this very second.

Tawly sprinted over to Twyjan, almost knocking the coffee over. Twyjan handed it over to Raynia and let Tawly bear-hug him. She then pulled away and hugged Raynia, who was beaming with pride (or something like it). She had a huge bouquet of daisies.

How does she know those are my favorite? Tawly thought, and then corrected her own self. *You couldn't keep a secret here to save your life*, she reminded herself. She looked sheepishly about wondering if everyone had read her mind and then they all laughed out loud.

She took the flowers from Raynia and hugged her warm body. Then Tawly noticed Zaduk standing over by the fire, quiet as usual. And right next to her, standing at attention, was Scout, eager as could be and waiting to be told he could go to Tawly. His ears were perked, and his eyes were fixed on her. When Zaduk gave the command, he came bounding across the room to Tawly. She motioned for him to jump up, and his front paws found her shins. He was still so little, so she knelt down to him. This allowed him to lay a big wet kiss on her neck. Everyone was laughing now. And then Scout seemed to catch a scent. He started whining like crazy. Everyone stopped and looked at Tawly. Scout could smell Janey on her. Tawly picked Scout up, lifted up his cute flappy ear, and took her first shot at speaking to an animal in the Next Place. Whatever she said, it must have worked, because the whining stopped. And Scout's tail started wagging, as if in anticipation of something really exciting that would happen. Tawly smiled and said out loud that she just couldn't tell him when.

With Scout by her feet, hot java in her hand, the white fire blazing in the background, and all her newfound friends from the Next Place surrounding her, Tawly began to feel at ease. She thought of her Janey, of course. But she knew Janey would be thrilled if she could see where Tawly was now. She let out a long sigh at the thought.

Once they had all sat down, Twyjan said, "You have a couple of days now, Tawly, to do with what you choose."

Tawly looked at him suspiciously and said, "You mean like a vacation?"

"Yes, indeed. Just that," Twyjan retorted.

"Well, I'm sorry, but that just seems weird to me. Here we are in this most amazing place; I have everything I need. I am surrounded by my new friends. I just cannot imagine where I would possibly want to get away to," Tawly said, thinking of those Sandals commercials she used to see on the tele back in the First Place.

Twyjan shook his head and said with a bit of exhaustion, "No, Tawly, not like the packaged, pre-planned vacations people take in the First Place. These are just days which are yours to do with what you choose. You might stay in bed and read all day if you so choose. But many choose to explore. You know, head to other Gathering Places, for example. Meet some of the others. Explore the lakes. Head to the mountains. Get lost on an island. Practice talking to the animals. Whatever. It is entirely up to you."

Tawly hemmed and hawed on this a bit as Raynia and Zaduk started discussing what was going on with them. Raynia had been called on by another Mender for help with a rather tricky predicament, and Zaduk was training another Teller. It seemed that someone was always helping someone else here. Tawly liked that. She looked over at Twyjan. He was, of course, reading her mind.

Tawly spoke: "So, what about you, Twyjan? What will you do with your vacation? I assume you have one since your sweet David is now safe."

Twyjan nodded his head and said, "Yes, I do, but I'm sticking around. Maybe selfishly because I want to see David after he is given his first role here. But also for Ike. I have the inside scoop from Annais that he thinks he will be a formidable Taker, and he hoped I would talk to him. He also happens to be heading to our Gathering Place."

Twyjan lit up at this last sentence. Tawly figured Twyjan would like a Taker friend. Even as different as they appeared. They obviously had forged a common bond in both wanting to save David, and both were partly responsible for doing so.

So Tawly would be on her own for vacation. She found this both nerve-wracking and exciting. She would maybe talk to Raynia or Zaduk for some ideas. For now, she figured she would take a walk with Scout. And try to remember every second of being with her daughter. Everyone seemed to be departing the impromptu party at this point. Everyone hugged and started their own way.

Twyjan stopped as he was headed out. And he said, "They did tell you that you can go back to see Janey one more time, yeah?"

18

Tawly

Tawly had jumped up from her seat when Twyjan had told her she could go back one last time; no one had to tell her twice. But then she had paused. She had thought about this precious chance and decided not to squander it while she was this tired. She also realized it was late in the evening. Janey might still be recovering from the whole experience. She might even still be on the floor, surrounded by all those pills, Tawly had figured. So instead, she decided to wait for Monday morning. On Monday, she thought, she could get a good long look at both Janey and Gwin.

When Monday morning rolled around, Tawly was the first person to arrive at Gwin's little school. She found a sentry of a pine tree to take cover behind. It was in a small grove of pine trees interspersed with the maples that were just getting their leaves. She had butterflies as her eyes searched for Janey's little black sedan. Tawly knew this was her last chance to visit Janey in the First Place. And consequently, it might be her last glimpse at little Gwin's budding life as a toddler. She thought back to two nights before and felt again the physical sensation of hugging her daughter. She knew this feeling was something she would not forget. It reminded her of all the time she and Janey had gotten to spend together in the First Place to begin with. She had not lost one of those memories, either.

As Tawly waited for Janey to arrive with Gwin, she recalled a conversation she and her daughter had had just before she had gotten really sick. Iris had known she was dying. Her daughter had not. But she had sensed that her mom had something on her mind.

And so Janey had asked her point blank: "Mom, are you scared of dying?"

They had been taking a walk along a road with a breath-taking view. They had admired the beauty of the hills together and had laughed about how much work it was to walk up the same. They had always gotten along like this: thick as thieves. But this question had caught Iris by surprise. She had grabbed her daughter's hand, not looking at her, but rather looking at the road in front of them both. And she had replied simply, "I am not afraid of dying, but I am afraid of what I will miss."

She knew that this had made her daughter sad. But she, too, had been quite sad about this part. She had lain awake at night, wondering what little Gwin would grow up to do, whom she would fall in love with, what she would look like, and mostly, if she would remember her grandma. Iris had known it was not all about her, but she hadn't been able to let go of this last question. Would her life have any meaning to Gwin at all?

But now, Tawly knew better, and she knew differently. She had seen that every single thing she had done had carried with her from the First Place to the Next Place. And that everything that she was then and now was critical to everything Janey was in the First Place, and consequently everything that Gwin could and would be in the First Place. There was no undoing it. They were actually eternally intertwined. Their lives were like a puzzle which was being put together each and every day. Tawly might not get to see Gwin's first boyfriend firsthand, but deep down she knew they would someday sit by a fire together, with coffee (if indeed little Gwin took after her in this small addiction), and discuss just this. There would be so much to share. No, she didn't know that Gwin would be perfectly safe. She didn't know that she wouldn't get snatched off the Road of the Taken.

She didn't know any of this. But she knew the people in the Next Place. They were relentless in their protection of those in the First Place. And Annais was tireless in his vigilance. No, there were no certainties, but Tawly had found that the Next Place was brimming with promise and hope. She loved it there.

She started thinking about Scout, who would be waiting for her when she got home ... and that elusive trip she was to take. And then she noticed the little black car. This morning, when it came around the corner, it was such a stark contrast to the first time Tawly had come back and had seen Janey driving. Then, she might have described Janey's car as a very short hearse. It had seemed so weighed down by the depressed driver. But now, it was almost comical to behold. Janey pulled in the driveway of the little school at what looked like 100 miles per hour. Tawly noticed she had one hand on the wheel and a cup of coffee in the other, splashing a bit of coffee on the dash as she hit the brakes and careened in the parking lot. Tawly also heard music and noticed that Janey and Gwin were both singing. It was some raucous Carrie Underwood song. They were smiling and laughing, and the car almost seemed to be bouncing along in their glee. Tawly could not have been more pleased.

She watched as Janey pulled the car up to the school, running over the curb a bit. The preschool teacher was standing at the door. Apparently, Janey and Gwin were the last to arrive. Janey jumped out and pulled little Gwin out of the car. There was oatmeal stuck to Gwin's face that her mom tried to swipe away. Tawly's heart melted at the way little Gwin looked up at her mom expectantly ... waiting for that good-bye kiss and a promise to return. And Tawly understood the way Janey watched as little Gwin lined up inside with the other three- and four-year-olds. She knew Janey had a hard time dropping Gwin off and that she wondered how her daughter's day without her would be. This was the same thing Tawly was wondering about her own daughter now.

But Tawly knew there was a time to let go. And so, as Janey climbed back in the car, Tawly took one really good long last look. And finally, she thought she might give her one last message before she let her go. The timing was so good. The sun was coming over the horizon just now, and Janey was pulling out of the parking lot, heading east. And so Tawly went quickly to work, painting the most stunning sunrise she could dream up. The sun burst out at just the right moment, through the gorgeous backdrop Tawly had painted. The gray of the lingering clouds and fog hung softly in front of the spring greens of the new grasses and budding trees. And the sun took on a blazing hot pink, which stole the show entirely. Janey stopped the car in the middle of the parking lot. The pink sky reflected on Janey's smiling face. Tawly stared at her daughter. As she stared she saw a young mother with a renewed sense of hope, basking in the little black sedan that was now flooded with cotton candy light, Tawly exhaled and closed her eyes. But just before they shut, she could have sworn that Janey looked right over at her.

Jane

I had sifted through my text messages the morning I woke up and had found only one person who had called me out on my drama: Elaina. As elusive and generic as I had tried to be with her, she had texted me back and said in her somewhat bossy manner:

I don't know what's going on, but we need to get together. Panera. Coffee. Monday. After we get the kids to school. Don't tell me no.

So, after I had collected myself and the stray pills, I had texted her back to agree. It was indeed Sunday, and Gwin's dad was bringing her home that afternoon. So I began to get ready for her arrival. I left the stuffed animal tea party as a tribute to my own survival. Gwin didn't need to know why they were celebrating. Once I had most everything in order, I had sat down on the bed. And then it had caught my eye: Iris's purple shawl, half-buried under my pillow. The memory had begun to form, and as I was drawn back to the scene where my mom and I had said goodbye, my heart began to flood with the sanctuary of her presence. My cells seemed to recall the experience of having been next to her and of having one more hug from her. I could still see us peering at each other over mugs of coffee … but where had we been? I wracked my brain but came up empty. And when Gwin got home, it all seemed rather far away. The rest of the day went by quickly. When it was time for bed, although I still covered myself with my mom's shawl, it felt more like I was being embraced and less like I was hiding away. On Monday, I opened my eyes and noted that the sinking sensation I had awoken with lately had shifted.

"Momma!" Gwin cried.

Slightly shaken, but slightly elated, I moved now with an ease I had not felt in the last few weeks and swung around the corner to meet my daughter's sleepy gaze. There was an involuntary inhale on my part as my face broke into an instantaneous smile, and Gwin, in an appropriately seismic response, leaped out of bed.

"Good morning, Momma!"

It was as if we had both just awoken: Her from her night's rest and me from some darker sort of sleep. I think her three-year-old spirit sensed an awakening in my own. We made our way to the kitchen, and as we pecked away at getting her ready for her day at preschool, bits and pieces of my time with my mom, whom I now sometimes remembered as Tawly, would flash into my head. As I poured Gwin's milk and got her gummy vitamins out, I tried to remember how I got there, how I got back, why I came back, or any of the other people who seemed to be lurking in the lack of my recollection. But nothing came. *Well,* I told myself, *I will work it all out. I'm sure it will all come back to me.* Or would it? I was unsure, so I reverted to cramming ziplocked portions of provision into Gwin's lunch bag.

As we edged out of our quaint little neighborhood, a school bus turned just in front of us. The mustardy yellowness of it in the early morning darkness struck me. Perhaps it was the contrast of that yellow against the dark gray March sky. Whatever it was, something was moving inside me. I tried to place my finger on it. And then I realized, I was experiencing the sense of happiness again. No matter if it was just the way the bus looked. Who cared? I actually felt happy. I couldn't believe it. I laughed. The blinders of despair seemed to be opening a tad. I looked in the rearview mirror. Gwin had the same look in her eyes. We had never physically looked a lot alike, but we were emotional twins. I could read her like a book.

Such an apropos saying, I thought. But then was unsure why I thought it.

Gwin was engrossed in the present moment. In a childlike fashion, she eyed her surroundings with wonder and astonishment, even something so simple as a mustard school bus on a grayish kind of day.

Yesterday, I would have envied how at ease she seemed. But today, I reveled in the same. I flipped the stale radio station to a Carrie Underwood CD I had in the changer, and we both started singing at the top of our lungs. I navigated us down the highway at a quicker quip than I had been driving lately.

Gwin noticed and said, "Momma, you are like a race car driver."

I laughed and touched on the brakes a little. *I didn't want to end up in the Next Place anytime soon,* I thought. *Wait, what? What was the Next Place?* I asked myself. Weird. No matter. I checked the clock; we would be just on time. Just how I liked it. I swung into the parking lot as all the other moms were pulling out and flew up onto the curb. I backed it down and took a deep breath. Gwin was grinning in the back seat. I got out, opened her door, wiped some oatmeal off her face, and then walked her into the lobby of that little brick school. Today, it seemed like the most beautiful building in the whole world. I watched her walk in and get hooked up on that crazy tow line they used to walk down the hall. As if a three-year-old might get lost in the empty hall. It all made me laugh today.

As a first-time mom, I always had what I thought was an over-the-top reaction when it came to dropping little Gwin off for care. Everyone had always told me: "She'll be okay. It's fine." I never believed that, though. Perhaps because I was not really fine with it. And since my mom had died, they almost had to pry her out of my hands. Yet today, I felt content. As I pulled away, I watched in my rearview mirror as she walked and talked to the teacher, head bobbing over a disproportionately smaller body.

Out of the windshield, as my focus shifted to where I was headed, I saw the sun coming up. It was as if I had never seen a sunrise before. It was the most astounding thing I had ever seen. I couldn't even move. I was the only parent left in the parking lot, and no other cars were leaving, so I just stayed. And then something else caught my attention: a beautiful pine tree amongst the maples. I had not noticed it before. It looked like it was hiding out amongst the other trees. Not only that, but I could have sworn someone was standing over there under that one pine tree. Although the sky was entirely neon pink, there was a golden glow under that pine tree. No matter, I thought. It had been a really intense couple of days. I was allowed to have some hallucinations.

I looked back at the sunrise. I was still keenly aware that my mom was gone from here. And I knew that my battle to live without her would be an uphill one. Yet the grip that grief had held over me for the past couple of months was not quite as strong as it had been. There was a new space in my heart that seemed open for promise, hope, and possibility. And if I closed my eyes, even in the middle of my little black sedan, imbued with the early morning pink sunrise, I could see her and feel her. I just couldn't figure out why she always seemed to be in some lodge, with a blazing fire, and a steaming cup of coffee in her hand.

CPSIA information can be obtained
at www.ICGtesting.com
Printed in the USA
FFOW03n0632120218
45030328-45382FF